"You did say I could call you," Caleb said

She shrugged dismissively. "So I changed my mind," she challenged.

Caleb resisted the impulse to lean forward and shake her. "So you did," he said heavily. "Running away from your emotions is never the answer, you know, Helen," he added softly.

Her eyes narrowed. He couldn't know about Daniel specifically, but he knew enough to realize someone had hurt her badly. "How I deal with the pain in my life is my business," she bit out.

"Not if it affects what's between us."

"There's nothing between us," she snapped, her guard well back in place now. "Physical attraction—"

"There's more to it than that, and you know it."

CAROLE MORTIMER, one of our most popular—and prolific—English authors, began writing in the Harlequin Presents series in 1979. She now has more than seventy selling romances to her credit and shows no signs whatever of running out of plot ideas. She writes strong traditional romances with a distinctly modern appeal, and her winning way with characters and romantic plot twists has earned her an enthusiastic audience worldwide.

Books by Carole Mortimer

HARLEQUIN PRESENTS

Don't miss any of our special offers. Write to us at the following address for information on our newest releases.

Harlequin Reader Service
P.O. Box 1397, Buffalo, NY 14240
Canadian address: P.O. Box 603,
Fort Erie, Ont. L2A 5X3

CAROLE MORTIMER

memories of the past

Harlequin Books

TORONTO • NEW YORK • LONDON
AMSTERDAM • PARIS • SYDNEY • HAMBURG
STOCKHOLM • ATHENS • TOKYO • MILAN
MADRID • WARSAW • BUDAPEST • AUCKLAND

For
Timothy Roy Faulkner Kershaw

Harlequin Presents first edition April 1992
ISBN 0-373-11451-6

Original hardcover edition published in 1991
by Mills & Boon Limited

MEMORIES OF THE PAST

CHAPTER ONE

'I'M THINKING of selling Cherry Trees,' Helen's father had told her.

Sell Cherry Trees, the house she had been born in, her home until she was nineteen, the place where her mother had, sadly, spent so many months of illness, before finally succumbing to that illness eight years ago. Sell the home that had meant so much to them all over the years? Never!

Of course, she didn't need two guesses as to who had put the unheard of before idea into her father's head. Caleb Jones. The man who actually wanted to buy Cherry Trees.

She had heard nothing but 'Cal Jones' this and 'Cal Jones' that since the man had moved on to the old Rawlings Estate six months ago. Her father seemed to think he was wonderful, had spent many an evening playing chess with him over the months, and so, consequently, he had talked a lot about Mr Caleb Jones during her regular Sunday evening telephone calls to him.

And she had made her own enquiries about the man. What she had learnt certainly hadn't endeared him to her. Or rather, it was what she *hadn't* learnt about him that bothered her so much.

She wasn't interested in the personal life of the man, although according to her father Caleb Jones was a cross between a saint and the Good Fairy, having taken on the guardianship of his young nephew after his parents had died. And his business dealings seemed to be a closed book. Or too much of an open book.

As a highly placed accountant in London, she had enough contacts in the business world to enable her to discreetly obtain the information she wanted. Oh, there was information enough, but it was all just a little too neat and tidy as far as she was concerned, Caleb Jones was either exactly what he appeared to be, a financial genius, or he was a crook. Nothing but one of the two extremes could have made possible the meteoric rise to the successful millionaire businessman that Caleb Jones was at only thirty-nine. And, despite her father's admiration for the man, Helen didn't believe it was the former.

A man like that wasn't going to buy Cherry Trees if she could possibly prevent it.

Which was why she was driving down to her home on the Hampshire coast for the weekend to try and dissuade her father from the idea.

Sell Cherry Trees!

She still couldn't believe her father was even considering it!

Caleb Jones had to have exerted some pressure, even if it was only that of supposed friendship, to have got her father to go even that far; he had always claimed in the past that he would never leave the house which, although once the old gatehouse of the Rawlings Estate, had been his home since he'd married her mother thirty years ago.

It was only since Caleb Jones moved on to the estate and began to work on him that he had even contemplated changing his mind. Well, he was about to find out that David Foster's daughter wasn't as gullible to his ruthless charm.

Not far to go now. She had been aware of the freshness of the sea air for some miles, had her side-window down in the heat of the July day, knew that she was even now turning down the narrow hedge-sided lane that edged one side of the Rawlings Estate.

It was a vast estate, comprised of thousands of acres, covered all of the land between here and the sea, was one of the last big private estates left intact in England. And now it all belonged to Caleb Jones.

Except the rambling old house that had once been its gatehouse.

Caleb Jones. Even the man's name conjured up visions of a Godfather-like figure, sitting back smugly among the luxury of the earnings that, on the surface, seemed to have been acquired too cleanly. Not that one of the people she had spoken to about him had made one derogatory remark or cast one suspicion on him. But it was this very lack of open maliciousness that made her so wary; in a business world like London that just wasn't natural. Not natural at all . . .

What the——?

Her foot moved desperately to the brake pedal as something wandered across the lane in front of the car. Her panic turned to complete horror as she realised it wasn't a small animal as she had first suspected, but a very small *baby* toddling along on unsteady legs!

She turned the wheel sharply to the left, badly shaken as the car came to a shuddering halt on the grass verge, turning quickly in her seat to see the baby picking itself up after a slight stumble, completely unaware of the narrow escape it had just had if its proudly pleased smile was anything to go by.

Helen quickly released her seatbelt and scrambled out of the car, her only thought now to scoop the baby up out of harm's way before another vehicle came innocently around the corner and perhaps didn't manage to avoid hitting the tiny dungaree-clothed figure.

Dark blue eyes widened indignantly as Helen lifted the baby up, the pink rosebud of a mouth setting mutinously at what was obviously an unwanted interruption to what had been turning out to be a great adventure.

Once she reached the side of the lane Helen found herself looking into a face so angelically beautiful that it gave her heart a jolt. Above the rose-bud mouth was a tiny button nose, and the dark blue eyes were fringed with long black lashes that fanned down against rosily healthy cheeks as the baby blinked up at her curiously.

Above the heart-shaped face was a riot of jet-black curls of such a length that it was difficult to tell whether the child was a boy or a girl. The dungarees were certainly no indication; children's clothes seemed to be unisex nowadays. And the parents could in no way be blamed for the indulgence of allowing the glossy black curls to grow so long even if it were a boy; it would be almost sacrilege even to think about cropping such a crowning glory.

But where *were* the parents? The child couldn't have walked that far on these unsteady little legs, and Helen knew from having lived here most of her life that there were no houses in the near vicinity. But she had to find the parents somehow, couldn't just drive off with the child and not——

'Sam? Sam! Lord, Sam, where the hell are you?'

Helen could hear the panic in the male voice, knew the still rebellious bundle squirming about in her arms had to be the missing 'Sam'.

'Over here,' she called out firmly, crossing the road in the direction of the voice.

The father. It had to be. The likeness between the two was unmistakable, the riotous dark curls, the dark blue eyes, the latter on the man anxious with the desperate worry he was obviously suffering at the disappearance of his child.

'Sam!' he gasped, having eyes for no one but the child. 'Thank heaven!' His face was pale, his hand shaking visibly as he ran it through his hair, running across the road, taking the eager child into his arms to bury his face in its throat, murmuring words of assurance and thanks for the baby's safe recovery.

Helen took advantage of these brief few minutes to take a closer look at the father. His hair was slightly wet to look at, the blue and black checked shirt he wore also appearing slightly damp, as if he had been exerting himself beneath the hot sun before the disappearance of his young child.

Well, whatever he had been doing at the time, he had no right to have been doing it when it had obviously distracted his attention from keeping the necessary watchful eye on his baby; she was still shaking from the horror of almost running the tiny child down!

The man, finally reassured that no bodily harm had befallen the child, looked up at Helen. 'I can't thank you enough——'

'Thank me!' Helen repeated harshly, breathing heavily in her agitation as delayed shock began to set in; she could have *killed* this adorable baby! 'What on earth were you doing allowing the child to wander off in that way?'

'Look, I understand you're upset——'

'Upset?' she cut in again, green eyes bright with anger. 'I don't think *upset* even begins to cover it,' she dismissed scathingly. 'I could have—could have——' She broke off shakily, breathing deeply. 'Don't you realise I actually had to swerve to avoid hitting the baby?' Her voice was slightly shrill.

The man paled again, turning slowly to look at her car parked at an awkward angle on the side of the road. 'I hadn't realised...'

'Obviously not,' she snapped.

'I was hedge-cutting when——'

'You had no right to bring a small child out here with you when you're working,' Helen reprimanded him incredulously, too disturbed herself at the moment to feel remorse for the way her bluntness had caused that almost grey tinge to the man's skin.

'I had him in a play-pen,' the man attempted to explain.

'Obviously not securely enough,' Helen bit out impatiently. 'And I'm sure your employer can't approve of your bringing such a young child to work with you.'

'I think I should explain, Miss——' Dark brows rose enquiringly over those deep blue eyes.

'Foster,' she supplied impatiently. 'Although I don't see what my name has to do with anything,' she dismissed coldly. 'I think your employer might be more interested to learn your name——'

'I should have realised immediately that you're David's daughter,' the man murmured thoughtfully, his eyes warm now. 'You have the same colouring, and he did mention that you might be coming down this——'

'The fact that you appear to have an acquaintanceship with my father doesn't alter for one moment the fact that I intend to see that nothing like this ever happens again.'

'You have to realise that it won't,' he protested cajolingly.

Helen's mouth firmed. 'I intend to see that it doesn't,' she told him coldly. 'You may be known to my father but so is Mr Jones—and I intend to inform him of your irresponsible behaviour at the earliest opportunity.'

'But——'

She held up one slender hand in a silencing movement. 'I don't want to hear any further excuses. For now I would suggest you take the baby home where it belongs, preferably leaving it with its mother, or at least someone with more sense than you appear to have——'

'But if you would just listen to me——'

'I don't think you have anything more to say that I would care to listen to,' she told him coldly. 'Now if you'll excuse me,' she added with haughty dismissal, 'I would like to complete my journey.' Her father was just expecting her some time today and wouldn't even realise she had experienced this delay, but she was feeling too sickened by the horrific accident that had almost occurred to want to talk to this man any more.

'Of course.' He nodded, looking more than abashed. 'I really am sorry for what happened. There must be a fault with the play-pen——'

'I would say it's more probable that the baby managed to climb out of it in some way,' she said disparagingly, one glance at the mischievous smile on the baby's angelically innocent face telling her the child was more than capable of doing such a thing.

The man glanced down at the baby too, the fingers on one tiny hand pulling playfully at the dark hairs on his chest. 'You could be right,' he agreed frowningly. 'I hadn't noticed any fault on the pen itself earlier, I just assumed... I'm beginning to realise it doesn't pay to assume anything with you, you little monkey!' He tickled the baby's tummy as he spoke, its shrill giggles quickly filling the air.

'I'll be on my way,' Helen told him abruptly, turning on her heel.

A hand on her arm stopped her just as she reached the car, and she looked up at the man with coolly questioning eyes.

'I really am grateful,' he said gruffly. 'If anything had happened to Sam...' He repressed a shudder. 'I couldn't have lived with myself.' He shook his head.

He wouldn't have been able to live with himself! Dear lord, if she had harmed one hair on that baby's head...

'Just think yourself lucky that I don't drive on this road often enough to risk speeding along it, otherwise we might have been having a vastly different conversation from this one!' With that final verbal reprimand Helen got back into her car, firmly closing the door behind her to restart the engine, just wanting to be on her way now that the crisis was over.

She took one final glance at father and baby in her driving mirror before she turned the corner and they were no longer in view.

Irresponsible man, to let a young child wander off in that way.

She still hadn't found out his name, but there couldn't be that many men in this area that her father knew with those looks and an adorable baby like Sam. She wasn't normally a person who interfered in other people's lives, mainly because she never welcomed any intrusion into her own life, but what had happened this afternoon had been too serious to ignore, let alone forget.

She hadn't relaxed at all by the time she had driven the two miles further on to Cherry Trees, turning in at the driveway of the mellow-bricked house, taking a few minutes after parking to just sit and look at her childhood home.

She never ceased to feel a warm glow whenever she came back to this house, probably because it had always been so much more to them all: the haven for her parents' marriage, her own warm cocoon of childhood, the garden and surrounding trees that had given the house its name having been her own private playground.

The house itself was low and rambling, the bricks a mellow sandstone, the windows and twin balconies on the second storey, either side of the front porch, newly painted, she noted.

She had no doubt her father had done the painting himself, despite her request for him not to do so after the last time two years ago when he had fallen off the ladder and broken his ankle. Nagging him didn't seem to get her anywhere, but she would have to mention it to him again anyway. Maybe just for once he might listen. He wasn't getting any younger, for goodness' sake, and it was about time he realised it!

As if her thinking about him had alerted him of her arrival her father stepped out of the house into the sunshine, and it was difficult at that moment to think of him as anything but young. The sunlight glinted on hair as golden blond as her own, his face still handsome and reasonably unlined despite his fifty-five years, his step jaunty, his body having retained the litheness of his youth.

'Going to sit out here all day?' he teased lightly, bending down to her open window. 'I saw you from the balcony in my bedroom,' he explained, frowning suddenly as he looked at her. 'How long have you been wearing your hair like that?'

Helen could hear the censure in his voice, one hand moving up instinctively to smooth the neat plait that reached halfway down her back, a feathered fringe lightly brushing her brow. With this coupled with her tailored navy-blue skirt and neat white blouse, she knew she looked very businesslike. But that had been exactly how she had wanted to look when she'd got ready this morning. That her father didn't like it she was left in no doubt.

'A few months,' she said dismissively, getting out of the car. 'The house is looking marvellous, you must——'

'I wish the same could be said for you,' her father cut in bluntly. 'You've lost even more weight. It isn't attractive, Helen.'

'Stop changing the subject, Daddy,' she reproved impatiently, knowing exactly what he was doing. 'You've been working on the house again when I specifically asked you not——'

'Cal had someone come over and do it,' he interrupted with steady patience.

Rather than being reassured by that information, Helen bristled resentfully. Oh, she was glad enough that her father hadn't done the painting after all, but that Caleb Jones should have had a hand in it . . .

'You should have told me it needed doing,' she said shortly. 'I would have arranged for someone to come in and do it.'

'I told you, there was no need to trouble you. Cal——'

'Caleb Jones obviously has his own reasons for wanting to keep this house up to a certain standard,' she bit out curtly, her eyes flashing. 'Which is precisely why I'm here, you know that.' She swung her case out of the boot of the car, her movements very precise in her agitation.

'And I thought you had come to see me,' her father said self-derisively.

She straightened abruptly, sighing her disapproval of his levity as she saw his eyes twinkling with amusement. 'This isn't a laughing matter, Daddy.' She shook her head.

'I couldn't agree more,' he grimaced. 'I haven't even had my kiss hello yet!'

Her cheeks coloured hotly at the gentle reprimand. 'I'm sorry, Daddy.' She kissed him warmly on the cheek. 'I had a horrible experience not fifteen minutes ago, and I don't think I can be thinking straight yet.'

Her father immediately looked concerned, demanding to know the full story, waiting until they were seated in the comfort of the lounge drinking a much-needed cup of tea. She could see her father was as horrified as she over what had almost occurred.

He looked disturbed. 'And the child's name was Sam, you say?'

'Mm,' she nodded, shrugging. 'I couldn't tell if it was a boy or a girl, only that it was adorable.' Her expression softened slightly at the thought of the tiny child.

'He's a cute little imp, all right,' her father mused. 'A real handful.'

Her eyes widened. 'You do recognise who I'm talking about, then?'

'Oh, yes.' He nodded, looking at her closely. 'Sam reminds me a little bit of Ben,' he said softly, the statement almost a query.

Helen felt herself stiffen. It was purely instinctive, and yet she couldn't help herself. Ben had been a long time ago. And yet she still couldn't talk about him, not naturally, the way that her father now could.

'Perhaps,' she dismissed tightly. 'But at the moment I'm more concerned with speaking to Mr Jones and making sure an incident like today never happens again.' She knew she sounded pompous and prim, but the incident had been too serious to simply ignore and try to forget about.

Her father nodded thoughtfully. 'Speaking to Cal should definitely ensure that.'

Helen looked at him frowningly, a little disturbed about the way he said that. 'I don't want to get this man into trouble, or anything like that. But you have to realise how dangerous his behaviour could have been.'

'Of course I can,' he agreed unhesitatingly. 'Cal will too.'

She didn't feel at all reassured by her father's attitude. 'He won't sack the man, will he?'

Her father raised blond brows. 'Would it bother you if he did?'

'Well, of course it would,' she snapped irritably. 'Jobs aren't all that easy to come by in this area, and the man obviously has a young family to support and look after.'

'He only has Sam,' her father put in quietly.

'Even so——'

'Cal will give him the roasting he deserves,' he said with certainty.

She had already done that, in no uncertain terms, and jobs *weren't* plentiful in this particular area. Besides, she could still see that adorable little face looking up at its father so trustingly...

After all, she had already told the man exactly what she had thought of the whole incident, and she could tell by the stricken look on his face how affected he had been by it all, so surely that constant memory of what might have happened was enough. It certainly wasn't likely to happen again, she was sure of it.

'Perhaps it isn't necessary to discuss it with Mr Jones after all,' she said lightly. After all, she had plenty of other things she needed to talk to Caleb Jones about—talking about today's incident would only confuse things! 'He doesn't really need to know about it,' she decided with finality.

'Hm,' her father said thoughtfully. 'There's only one thing wrong with that, darling.'

'Yes?' she prompted sharply, not seeing what the complication was at all.

He nodded. 'Cal already knows what happened this afternoon.'

'You mean the man will have told him about it himself?' Helen frowned at the thought of the man's having gone to him so quickly.

'Cal *is* the man, darling,' her father explained huskily. 'Sam is the nephew I told you about, the one he's become guardian to. And I've invited Cal over to dinner tonight, so I'm sure he will want to talk to you again about what happened.'

CHAPTER TWO

CALEB JONES. How on earth could Helen have guessed *that* was Caleb Jones?

She had questioned her father's certainty on the man she had met at the roadside's possibly being Caleb Jones, describing him in great detail, only to have her father insist it had been him, that the adorable toddler was definitely the nephew he was guardian to.

The man she had met hadn't looked thirty-nine, early thirties at the most, and he hadn't appeared anything like the cynically hardened businessman she had expected. She couldn't even imagine him in a suit and tie, and his hair was far too long to be considered 'respectable'! But he had been resident on the estate most of the last six months, so that could possibly account for the untidiness of the latter.

But even so, it was hard to imagine that man with the overlong black hair, unlined face and muscled body as anything but the labourer she had first taken him to be.

And he was coming here to dinner tonight, before she had even had the chance to talk to her father about his idea of selling Cherry Trees!

Not that she doubted for a moment that the ploy had been deliberate on her father's part, at least. He had been deliberately evasive on the subject since her arrival, carrying her case upstairs for her and insisting she must feel in need of a shower after her journey. She did feel hot and sticky, but the shower could have waited for a while, except that her father obviously had other ideas.

She could already tell he was going to be at his most stubborn this weekend!

Which was precisely why she had got herself ready for dinner early; she was determined she would talk to her father about selling the house before Caleb Jones arrived.

He was in the lounge pouring himself a pre-dinner drink when she got downstairs, as she had known he would be. There was nothing her father enjoyed more than half an hour or so's leisurely relaxation with a glass of good whisky before he was due to eat.

He looked surprised to see Helen down so early, although there was none of the censure in his eyes for what she was wearing that there had been earlier. The classic plain black dress that moved silkily about her body as she walked was one of her father's favourites. And she knew that, but if he wanted to play at being devious so would she!

She had styled her hair in a much softer style for him too, soft curls piled loosely on top of her head, several loose tendrils on her forehead and cheeks framing her face.

'A definite improvement.' He stood up to pour Helen a sherry, eyeing her mischievously. 'Cal will like the change too, I'm sure.'

She bristled angrily. 'I really don't care what Mr Jones likes, as I'm sure you well know,' she reproved, accepting her sherry and sitting down in an armchair. 'And the reason I looked the way that I did when I arrived was because I had been to work this morning and drove straight down here from the office.' And her father was one of the few people she would ever have bothered to explain herself to in this way.

But then, he had obviously known her all her life, and it was a little difficult to stand on your dignity with someone who had changed your nappies for you as a baby, seen you with your two front teeth missing, reassured you that those detested freckles on your nose would disappear one day—although he had been wrong about that—comforted you through your first bout of unrequited love!

He made himself comfortable in the chair opposite her. 'How is the big city?' he drawled, his eyes still twinkling, not the clear green of

Helen's but a marvellous hazel colour that made them change from brown to green to blue. Though he was in his mid-fifties, and despite the devastating sadness of losing Helen's mother so early in their lives together, they hadn't lost any of their glow.

Helen eyed him derisively, not fooled for a minute. 'The "big city" is fine,' she returned drily. 'And stop being evasive.'

'Evasive?' His eyes widened innocently. 'Me? I don't know what you mean.'

'Oh, Daddy,' she smiled wryly, 'you really are a terrible liar.'

He gave a deep sigh, giving up all pretence. 'It's my house, Helen——'

'But it's my home,' she cut in protestingly.

He gave her a chiding look. 'It's seven years since you left here; London is your home now.'

She shook her head firmly. 'I always think of Cherry Trees as my home.'

'Really?' he returned drily. 'And how many times have you visited the place during the last year, the last six months, in fact?' His brows were raised questioningly.

Colour heightened her cheeks at the softly spoken reprimand. She had been down to the house twice in the last year, the last time being at Christmas seven months ago; if she had been here during the last six months she would have recognised the danger of Caleb Jones earlier, and perhaps have been able to put a stop to it before it got this far!

'It's still home, Daddy——'

'It's a big, rambling old house with lots of memories and the hunger for children's laughter to fill the rooms once again,' he cut in harshly. 'And, as you've assured me on several occasions that you'll never move from London now because it's where your work is, that you have no intention of marrying or having children, the likelihood of your one day being able to bring my grandchildren down to visit me sometimes seems very remote!'

Helen flinched at the hard accusation in his voice. She knew her father didn't mean to be deliberately cruel, but nevertheless his words cut into her like a barb.

'It's your *home*,' she began firmly.

'Cal has promised me a cottage on the estate so that I can still stay in the area,' her father dismissed that problem.

'*Cal* seems to have thought of everything, doesn't he?' she said tautly.

'It's only logical——'

'As far as *he's* concerned it's only logical,' Helen cut in scathingly. 'But at the end of the day our home will have been sold and Caleb Jones will own it! It's all very neat and tidy—in his favour.'

Her father sighed. 'I've already explained that the arrangement suits me too.'

Well, it didn't suit her! As far as she was concerned Caleb Jones had used his friendship with her father—if indeed that was really what it was—to talk him into something that would, in the long run she was sure, be completely wrong for him. Her father loved this house, and she knew he would regret leaving it almost as soon as the deed had been done.

'We'll see,' she bit out tightly.

'There's nothing to see, Helen.' He shook his head. 'I've already made my mind up to sell the house.'

And she was here to undo it. He was being influenced by his feelings of good will towards Caleb Jones, and the other man was obviously taking advantage of that. Caleb Jones might not look like a cynically hardened businessman, but he obviously knew how to behave like one! Maybe it was that very contradiction that had made it possible for him to be so successful!

'That will be Cal now.' Her father beamed his pleasure as he stood up to answer the ring of the doorbell. He paused at the door. 'I hope this is going to be a pleasant evening, Helen.'

She wished she could assure him that it would be, but they must all be aware that at best it was going to be a strain, at worst impossible. And with her father thinking so highly of Caleb

Jones, and her own suspicions about the other man, it could so easily become the latter.

She could hear the murmur of the two men's conversation out in the hallway as her father brought the other man through to the lounge, deciding she would be at less of a disadvantage if she stood up to greet their guest; she really wasn't that tall, only five feet five inches, but the tailored clothes and neat hairstyle she wore for work gave the impression that she was much more imposing than she was. Tonight she only had the advantage of two-inch heels on her shoes, and as Caleb Jones was well over six feet tall he would still dwarf her.

She stood over by the patio doors that led out into the garden, knowing that from this position she had a clear view of Caleb Jones as he entered the room, but that the shadows in this alcove in early evening would mean it took him a few seconds to locate her.

It seemed a slightly childish move on her part, and yet as Caleb Jones stepped into the lounge ahead of her father she was glad she had taken it. The man looked devastatingly attractive in a dark lounge suit and the palest of green shirts, his dark hair brushed into some sort of order this evening, although it was still too long to be considered fashionable.

But with presence such as this man had he didn't need to be fashionable! She could recognise that air of authority for what it was now, although she doubted that in his privileged position he very often needed to enforce it.

He came towards her unhesitatingly, not seeming to have needed to have sought her out at all, knowing where she was instinctively. 'Miss Foster.' He held out his hand.

'Her name is Helen, and yours is Cal,' her father cut in firmly.

'Yes, please do call me Helen,' she invited, revealing none of the disturbance she felt as her hand was taken firmly in Caleb Jones's much larger one. His grip was firm and cool, and just long enough to be remembered. 'May I say you're looking slightly better now than you did this afternoon?' she added with a softness that was designed to take some of the sting out of her words.

The man in front of her didn't even blink at her deliberate reminder of their first meeting. 'I feel a lot better than I did this afternoon,' he returned evenly.

He knew of her antagonism, Helen could tell that as surely as if the words had already been spoken between them. As they surely must be some time very soon. But not in front of her father; she could already sense that this man had already decided that whatever the problem was it would be kept strictly between themselves. And that suited her just fine; she didn't want her father upset unduly unless she could help it either.

'And Sam?' her father put in affectionately. 'How is he?'

Caleb Jones's expression softened at the mention of the baby. 'The same little devil as usual,' he mused. 'He isn't even aware of the near catastrophe he caused.' He turned back to Helen. 'You were right about "the great escape", by the way. The little devil had piled his toys up in one end of his play-pen and used them to climb over the side,' he explained.

'He's very bright for his age.' Helen's father shook his head ruefully.

And so like Caleb Jones to look at—the thought popped unbidden into Helen's mind. And she instantly questioned it. Of course if Sam was his nephew that would explain their similarity, but there could also be a more obvious explanation. This second explanation might also explain why Caleb Jones had chosen to buy the estate in the first place and bury himself down here far away from London where his offices were. She didn't usually have such a suspicious mind, but her ambivalent feelings towards Caleb Jones had been aroused from the first.

It would also be much easier to understand his taking on the guardianship of such a young baby if the child were his own.

She hadn't taken too much interest in his private life when she had been making enquiries about him, except to know that he was unmarried. But that didn't preclude his having a child, a child that he might want to protect from the public eye. Not that it was really anyone's business but his own, and Sam *was* adorable...

'Very,' Caleb Jones agreed with her father indulgently. 'Too bright for his own good sometimes,' he grimaced. 'I'm beginning to wonder which one of us is in control of the situation.'

Helen's father chuckled. 'Why Sam is, of course. All children are. The secret is not to let them ever realise that. I remember when Helen and——'

'Daddy, shouldn't you be checking on dinner?' she cut in pointedly; the last thing she needed was her father reminiscing to this man about her childhood!

Her father gave her a knowing look, but his answer was directed towards the other man. 'Never become a father, Cal,' he said self-derisively, moving to the door. 'They grow up and start treating you as if *you're* the child!'

'I think it's a bit late for me to worry about that,' Caleb Jones said ruefully. 'Sam already has me taped.'

His beautiful mischievous nephew was another subject Helen would have preferred not to discuss if she could avoid it. But as her father left the room to check on their meal she knew their conversation was rather limited!

'Would you like a drink, Mr Jones?' she offered politely.

'A small whisky would be fine,' he accepted just as politely.

She moved smoothly across the room to pour the alcohol into a glass for him.

'Are you not joining me?' He raised dark brows enquiringly.

'I only drink wine,' she explained coolly. 'And I prefer to wait until we have our meal.'

Caleb Jones lowered his long length into an armchair before taking an appreciative sip of the neat alcohol. 'I've heard such a lot about you from David,' he explained. 'It's good to finally meet you at last.'

Helen looked at him scathingly. 'Is it?'

He didn't appear in the least perturbed by her manner. 'David obviously misses you very much,' he nodded.

She bristled angrily at what she sensed was a softly spoken reprimand. 'All children leave home to make a life for themselves at some time, Mr Jones,' she snapped.

'True,' he acknowledged without rancour.

Helen felt extremely irritated by the way he had made her feel guilty and then dropped the subject as if it were of no real importance. And it had been too smoothly done not to have been deliberate. Those innocently wide blue eyes were definitely deceptive, and she was more sure than ever that her preconceived idea of this man as being shrewdly clever was correct.

'How do you like——?'

'Could we dispense with the polite conversation when my father isn't around, Mr Jones?' she cut in caustically. 'We both know the reason I'm here, and polite chit-chat isn't going to gloss over that.'

He arched dark brows. 'I thought you were here to visit your father.'

'And I have already had this conversation with him earlier,' she snapped. 'With much more effect, believe me,' she added scornfully.

He gave an inclination of his head. 'I'm glad to hear it.'

She drew in a controlling breath at the censure in his voice. He least of all had the right to stand in judgement of her behaviour. 'At least my affection for my father is genuine,' she challenged softly.

He didn't move, not so much as a muscle, and yet Helen could feel the anger emanating from him. 'Implying?' he prompted tautly.

'Implying that——'

'Dinner is served,' her father announced lightly as he came back into the room, his eyes narrowing shrewdly as he sensed the antagonism flowing between his daughter and his friend. 'Let's go and eat before it all spoils,' he added distractedly.

He was upset by the tension between herself and the man he considered a close personal friend, Helen could tell that, and yet she couldn't do or say anything to put his mind at rest. She didn't trust Caleb Jones, and there was no use pretending, not even for one evening, that she did.

It couldn't be of any comfort to her father now, but he was actually the one who had always told her to be honest in her dealings with people, polite but honest. And that was exactly what she intended being with Caleb Jones.

'You don't cook, Helen?' a lightly mocking voice enquired as they all went through to the dining-room.

Her father chuckled his enjoyment, eyeing her teasingly.

'Yes, I cook, Caleb.' She knew the complete formality of 'Mr Jones' was out now that her father was back with them, but she stubbornly refused to call this man 'Cal'. 'But when I'm home my father insists on feeding me up; he doesn't think I look after myself properly in London,' she added drily.

'And do you?' the other man challenged softly.

Her mouth firmed. 'As well as any person living alone,' she bit out.

Caleb Jones nodded. 'I've lived alone in London myself—it's far from being an ideal situation.'

Helen couldn't help wondering just how often he had actually 'lived alone'.

But she couldn't help sensing yet another underlying criticism. 'It may have escaped your notice, Caleb,' she snapped, 'But there aren't too many vacancies for accountants in a rural area like this one!'

Once again he appeared unruffled by her vehemence. 'Strange you should mention that...' he murmured thoughtfully.

Helen didn't see anything in the least strange about it. This was a country area, with one or two small towns nearby, but none of them possessed the sort of company she wanted to be associated with. Up until now her father had always accepted that the move to London was necessary for the advancement of her career. She would not appreciate it if this man had been putting other ideas into his mind!

Her eyes flashed her anger. 'I don't see anything strange about it——'

'Oh, I didn't mean strangely odd,' Caleb Jones cut in smoothly. 'I meant what a strange coincidence; I'm looking for an accountant at the moment—in fact I'm going to start seeing people concerning that this week.'

Helen stared at him. 'You want an accountant working down here with you?'

He nodded. 'I spend most of my time here now, and rather than move all my staff and offices down here—which wouldn't please them, I'm sure—I thought a personal-assistant-cum-accountant liaising between here and London would be the perfect answer to the problem,' he explained lightly.

Helen had become more and more tense as he spoke, turning slowly now to look at her father, sure from his innocent expression—and his friendship with Caleb Jones—that he had known of the vacancy long before now.

And that too-innocent expression gave her a deep feeling of unease.

Surely her father hadn't expected her to be interested in applying for the job!

CHAPTER THREE

'YOU can't have been serious, Daddy,' Helen complained incredulously.

Dinner was long over, Caleb Jones had taken his leave a short time ago, and the two of them were enjoying a cup of coffee before going to bed.

Helen had lost her equilibrium somewhat after she had realised her father had seriously contemplated the idea of her working for Caleb Jones.

At the time she had passed the moment off with a flippant comment about liking her job in London, but she had known from her father's expression that he intended to pursue the subject once they were alone. Helen had decided that attack was the better form of defence!

Her father didn't appear in the least perturbed. 'It's an ideal step up the ladder for someone in your position,' he reasoned lightly.

'It's a leap,' she acknowledged self-derisively.

'Well, then——'

'Too much of a leap, Daddy,' she derided.

'I'm sure Cal would——'

'I certainly don't want any favouritism from him, thank you,' she snapped.

Her father looked annoyed by her outburst. 'I wasn't talking about favouritism, damn it——'

'Then what else would you call it?' she challenged, her cheeks red.

He drew in a controlling breath. 'Cal would merely consider your application as fairly as any others he receives.'

'I don't want to be "considered"——'

'I wish you would forget your prejudice of the man, and think what a really good opportunity it would be for you to work for him——'

'I don't *want* to work for him!' she cut in exasperatedly. 'I find the man totally obnoxious, and on top of that I question his ethics.'

'Helen!'

She had gone too far with her last remark as far as her father was concerned, she could see that, and yet it wasn't just Caleb Jones's underhand dealings over Cherry Trees that bothered her about the man; she still didn't know enough about him professionally to trust him completely in that area either.

'The City is suspiciously quiet about him,' she insisted. 'I would need to know a lot more about him than I do now before I would even consider working for him.'

'Don't let one bad experience sour you, Helen,' her father advised softly.

Colour warmed her cheeks at this gentle reminder of her youthful folly.

She had been extremely vulnerable when she'd first moved to London, had kept herself very much to herself during those first few years, so that by the time she'd taken up her position as a junior accountant in one of the larger firms she had been ripe for the attentions of a more senior accountant with the company.

It had taken her several months to realise that, while Daniel's personal investments weren't exactly illegal, they were at the very least unorthodox. And she had only found that out because by this time he had believed them to be close enough for her to be taken partly into his confidence, to suggest that she might like to supplement her own income in the same way.

It had been the end of what she had believed to be a promising relationship, and also the last time she had dated anyone in her own profession. The last time she had dated anyone at all, her father would have accused, but that wasn't strictly accurate; she did occasionally go out to dinner or the theatre if she met anyone she thought might be interesting to spend an evening with. But she had to admit those times were few and far between, and she rarely repeated the experience.

'I haven't, Daddy,' she assured him softly. 'I just find more satisfaction from my career than I do in a relationship with a man.'

'That's simply because you haven't met the right man yet,' he insisted.

'And have no interest in doing so for some time. If ever!'

'Then you should at least be interested in this position with Cal,' he reasoned.

Professionally she knew that she should, that she was, but personally she knew she would never be able to work for Caleb Jones. And besides, she hadn't just been making excuses when she'd said it was too big a leap for her professionally; Caleb Jones would need a very senior accountant indeed to handle the job he was talking of.

'It would have meant you could move back here,' her father put in pointedly.

And he would have no reason to sell Cherry Trees; she had already realised that. But she knew, even if her father didn't, that that had to be the last thing Caleb Jones wanted. Which meant her chances of getting the job were nil before she even started. She wouldn't humiliate herself by even trying!

'I enjoy my work in London, Daddy,' she told him firmly. 'I have no intention of leaving it.'

'I see,' he said flatly.

Helen sighed. 'No, you don't, but then you don't want to.'

'I just want—— Oh, never mind what I want,' he dismissed irritably. 'I can see I'm just wasting my breath.'

'Playing the martyr doesn't suit you, Daddy,' she told him drily.

An unaccustomed flash of anger darkened his eyes. 'You are the most stubborn, annoying—I can't believe you're a child of mine!'

She chuckled as she stood up. 'Strange— everyone, including you, has always said I'm exactly like you.'

He gave her a glowering look. 'Don't be so damned facetious!'

She grinned at him, her eyes glowing deeply green in her amusement. 'And I'm too old for that to work any more either!'

'More's the pity,' he mumbled, disgruntled.

Helen gave a leisurely stretch. 'Why don't we talk about all this again in the morning? It's been a long day and it's late.'

'And nothing will have changed by tomorrow,' he said ruefully. 'But I see your point about the time.' He stood up with a sigh. 'I'm feeling a little tired myself.'

In truth he did look slightly strained; he had lines about his eyes and mouth that she hadn't noticed earlier. Could it be that her father was finally beginning to show his years? Or was it something more than that? She felt pangs of guilt for not noticing the subtle changes earlier. And were they changes that Caleb Jones had seen and recognised? If they were he was being doubly underhand!

She looked at her father with concern. 'Are you feeling all right, Daddy?'

His ready smile erased the lines of strain, making Helen wonder if she could have merely imagined they were there at all. Her father was probably just tired after all.

'Never felt better,' he assured her. 'I always feel more cheerful when you come home for the weekend.'

'Daddy!' she reproved ruefully. Would he never give up?

He grinned. 'I've never claimed to be anything but a devious old devil.'

No, he hadn't, Helen mused as she prepared for bed. But he had overstepped his limitations this time. There was no way she was going to give up her job in London and come back down here to live. Maybe she was being selfish, but it was no use pretending she felt any differently.

She certainly wouldn't want to live permanently anywhere near Caleb Jones!

* * *

'Restful, isn't it?'

Helen turned sharply at the sound of that softly spoken voice.

Her father had gone off into town on some errand or other, and she had taken the opportunity to stroll along the beach near the estate; it had once been a place she had spent many soothing and calming hours.

And it had, in recent years, always been somewhere she had come to alone...

Caleb Jones standing several feet away, his bare feet planted firmly in the golden sand, bronzed legs revealed by the white shorts, a pale blue short-sleeved shirt completely unbuttoned down the front showing a chest that was just as tanned, was not a welcome intrusion into her solitude.

Far from it!

'I always thought so,' she replied pointedly.

In fact she had been immensely enjoying the gentle lap of the waves on the sand, her feet bare as she enjoyed the latter's coolness near the water's edge.

The local people from the village rarely used this beach, a much more popular one, with a few amenities like a small café, situated just around the bay. It shouldn't have surprised her in the least that Caleb Jones had discovered and invaded this quiet stretch of water; he seemed to have intruded on several other important parts of her life too!

His mouth quirked into a half-smile, and Helen was sure he knew exactly what she was thinking. His next words confirmed it. 'I always come here when I feel like being alone,' he drawled.

'No Sam today?' she challenged.

Caleb shrugged. 'He's taking a nap. His idea of the start of day is daybreak, so by this time he's ready for a sleep. So am I, come to that,' he added self-derisively.

'Don't you have him trained not to wake you yet?' Helen couldn't help her curiosity about the child she had met so precipitately.

He grimaced. 'That's a little difficult; his nursery is right next to my bedroom. And playing in his cot only lasts for a few minutes once he's woken up. After the last episode I'm loath to leave him anywhere on his own too long; lord knows what he would get up to!'

Helen frowned. 'Doesn't his nanny——?'

'I don't have a nanny for Sam,' he cut in quietly, bending down to pick up a pebble and skim it across the clear water in front of them.

His action gave Helen a few seconds to take in his surprising statement. If he didn't have a nanny for the little boy then that must mean... Good grief, wasn't that taking his guardianship of Sam just a little too far? After all, there couldn't be many men in his financial position who would even think of doing such a thing, let alone carry it out.

'That seems a little—ambitious,' she dismissed coolly.

No wonder he rarely spent time in London any more if he had taken on the full-time care of a very young child!

He raised dark brows mockingly. 'Because I'm a man?'

Her cheeks warmed at his taunting tone. 'Not necessarily,' she answered defensively. 'Bringing up a child is difficult for anyone, but for a man alone, a man with a full-time career to think of, I would have thought it was virtually impossible.'

'It's—hard, at times,' Caleb admitted. 'Hence the need for the PA.'

Helen stiffened, at once wary. 'Wouldn't it have just been easier to engage a nanny for the baby?'

'Easier, perhaps,' he conceded consideringly. 'But not half as much fun!'

He sounded as if he was really enjoying caring for the baby, and she had no reason to think otherwise; after all, he did seem to have changed his whole lifestyle to suit his new responsibilities. But even so, she still found it an odd thing for him to have done, especially when the child supposedly wasn't even his own.

'I wish you luck with your other venture,' she told him dismissively, hoping he would go away and she could be left alone to her thoughts—and the privacy of the beach!

He gave her a sideways glance, standing next to her now. 'Not thinking of applying yourself?'

She gave him a knowing look. 'There wouldn't be much point, would there?'

'No?'

He didn't give anything away, she would give him that! 'No,' she drawled derisively.

'Your father would like it.'

Her mouth twisted. 'But you and I know it's a foregone conclusion that it will never happen.'

'We do?'

'Of course,' she snapped, impatient with his evasive tactics. 'If you gave me the job it would mean my father wouldn't sell Cherry Trees to you.'

'Yes?'

'Well, we both know you don't want that to happen.' Her eyes flashed.

'Do we?'

'Don't start playing games with me, Mr Jones,' she bit out disgustedly. 'We both know that, for reasons of your own, you have decided to have Cherry Trees back as part of the estate, and my moving back here to live would certainly defeat that objective.'

He nodded slowly. 'Yes, I can see that it would,' he said thoughtfully.

His calm dismissal of the subject annoyed her even more. 'I think you should know right now that I have every intention of stopping you from ever having Cherry Trees!' Angry colour burned her cheeks. 'It's my family home; you don't need it for your damned estate.'

Dark blue eyes looked at her coolly. 'It was part of the original estate.'

'That doesn't mean it has to revert back to it,' she said heatedly.

'Your father seems to feel differently,' he pointed out calmly.

'My father is influenced by your supposed friendship,' she scorned. 'I'm not taken in so easily.'

Caleb gave her a long considering look. 'No,' he finally replied. 'I don't think that you are.'

'Believe it,' she snapped. 'I intend to stay down here for as long as it takes to convince my father he is making a mistake.'

'Oh?' He looked surprised. 'I thought you were only down for the weekend.'

'I can easily arrange to stay for longer,' she bit out.

In fact, she hadn't intended anything of the sort when she'd first come down, but after meeting Caleb Jones, and talking to her father, she had a feeling it was going to take much

longer than the weekend to make her father see
sense.

Caleb didn't look concerned. 'I'm sure your
father will like that.' He nodded distractedly,
glancing at his wristwatch. 'I'd like to continue
this conversation, Helen,' he smiled, humour
giving his eyes a dark glow, 'but I'm afraid I'm
expecting Sam's grandparents down for the
day,' the smile disappeared, his eyes grim, 'and
it wouldn't do to be late for their arrival.'

Helen looked at him closely. He didn't sound
at all thrilled about having his parents visit.
Maybe they didn't approve of him either!

'Don't let me keep you,' she mocked.

He nodded. 'I expect I'll see you again soon.'

She expected he would. She would have to
return to London for a couple of days, of
course, but she was due some holiday so she
intended being back as soon as possible. It
would just be a case of persuading her father
not to do anything until she came back. *Just*
a case? He could be so stubborn and head-
strong when he felt like it!

'Enjoy your weekend,' Caleb added softly,
turning to leave.

Before battle commences, Helen silently
added. Because a battle it most certainly would
be.

Odd, but she felt strangely elated at the
thought of it.

CHAPTER FOUR

'SOMETHING wrong, love?'

A ghost from the past.

But it couldn't have been, Helen instantly dismissed. She had to have imagined the familiarity of that handsome face of the driver of the sports car she had just passed in the lane on her way to Cherry Trees; Daniel believed the countryside was at the very least an alien planet!

Helen smiled brightly at her father as she got out of the car. It had taken her longer than she had thought to organise the breathing space she felt was necessary to sort out the problem of her father's decision to sell Cherry Trees. So it was now almost two weeks later—and a promise from her father not to do anything rash in her absence!—that she had managed to return home with the knowledge of two clear weeks' holiday in front of her. Surely two weeks would be long enough to persuade her father not to sell, and, more important than that, to convince Caleb Jones that her father *wouldn't* sell.

'It's good to be home,' she told her father with genuine warmth.

He grinned at her. 'Starting your campaign already?'

She moved briskly around the car to take her luggage from the boot. 'Not at all,' she dismissed. 'How is our esteemed neighbour?'

'Cal?' Her father sobered a little. 'He's all right, I suppose.'

Helen looked up at him searchingly. 'What's that supposed to mean?'

Her father shrugged. 'Nothing, really. Come on, let's go inside. It will be like old times, having you here again for a while.'

That was what she was hoping for. And she was more than willing to drop the subject of Caleb Jones for the moment, still shaken by that driver's resemblance earlier to Daniel. She hadn't seen him for years, their lifestyles completely different, but she still couldn't help shuddering every time she realised the narrow escape she had had with him. Every blond-haired Adonis was apt to remind her of what a fool she had been for the few months she had imagined herself in love with him.

'Starting *your* campaign already?' she returned just as mischievously as he had a few minutes earlier.

He raised blond brows. 'Well, at least this time you came home dressed for the occasion.'

He looked appreciatively at the casual white trousers and white T-shirt she wore, her hair secured loosely at her nape.

The ploy had been deliberate, Helen had to acknowledge mentally. She was genuinely looking forward to this visit with her father, but she also wanted it to go well for purely selfish reasons. No, they weren't selfish, she really believed her father would be unhappy living anywhere else but Cherry Trees. It was up to her to help him to realise that.

'I'm on holiday,' she dismissed lightly.

'You're at home while you have time off work,' her father corrected reprovingly. 'One hardly goes home for a holiday,' he derided drily.

She raised her eyes heavenwards, her mouth twisting wryly. 'That's very good, Daddy,' she taunted. 'But I merely meant I have time away from work to do as I please.'

'Of course you did,' he mocked.

'Daddy,' Helen sobered, 'I hope we aren't going to keep sparring like this the whole time I'm here——'

'Why not?' He grinned. 'I find it quite entertaining.'

'But very tiring.'

He shrugged. 'It makes life a lot more interesting, though.'

'If you say so,' she grimaced. 'But I don't intend giving you the satisfaction of baiting me every five minutes or so.'

'Oh, well,' he dismissed. 'It was fun while it lasted.'

And it was far from over, despite what she had said, and they both knew that!

'Anyway, you'll have someone else to "spar" with this evening.' He gave her a sideways glance.

Helen gave him a considering look; he was about as subtle as a blow between the eyes! 'Expecting a visitor tonight, are you?' she said as casually as she was able. Really, her father wasn't even waiting for her to get settled in before challenging her with Caleb Jones's presence in the house!

He shrugged. 'Only Cal for our usual Friday night game of chess. We cancelled the chess in favour of dinner the last time you were here out of consideration for you,' he explained lightly.

'How nice,' she said with saccharine sweetness.

'I thought so.' Her father grinned, not fooled for a moment.

He was impossible! But more like his old self this visit, Helen decided as they lingered over a meal of salad and fresh fruit. The lines of strain seemed less about his eyes and mouth today, the former having most of their usual mischievous glow.

But, despite her ready acceptance of Caleb Jones's expected arrival here tonight when she had only just arrived, it was really just another reminder of how close the two men had become these last months. And of how difficult it was going to be to place the wedge in the relationship that was going to be necessary to persuade her father just how deviously the other man was behaving.

Considering how warmly the two men greeted each other later that evening, that wasn't going to be easy to do!

'Nice to see you again, Helen.' Cal held out his hand in friendly greeting.

Tonight he was dressed in fitted denims that showed the narrowness of his hips and thighs, and a loose short-sleeved shirt of the same shade of blue as his eyes. With his overlong dark hair slightly wind-swept by the light breeze outside, and his eyes warmly smiling, he looked devastatingly attractive. As attractive as he had the first time she had seen him, before her knowledge of his identity had put her on her guard.

Remembering the last time she had seen him, she couldn't help thinking of the beautiful baby he had in his care.

'...doesn't bite, you know, Helen,' she heard her father mock lightly.

She blinked at him questioningly, blushing furiously as she realised Cal still had his hand extended in greeting, and she had been so lost in her own thoughts she hadn't even noticed it!

'I was wondering how your nephew is,' she said briskly as she lightly brushed her hand against his. Even that contact felt like too much, her hand seeming to burn where they had touched. She didn't need a complication like that, certainly not with this man!

She couldn't remember the last time she had been physically attracted to a man—yes, she could, and look at the chaos Daniel had almost caused in her life. Caleb Jones could wreak absolute havoc! She must be having a brainstorm to have even been thinking of him in that way, must need this holiday more than she had realised. She would *not* fall for this man's charm, as others seemed to do so easily.

'Have you left him in the care of the maid again?' she added caustically, meeting his gaze with defiant challenge.

His mouth tightened, his eyes taking on a grim look. 'As a matter of fact——'

'Helen, how about making a drink for Cal and me?' her father interrupted, his brows raised warningly as she opened her mouth to protest at this abrupt interruption to her conversation with Cal.

She glanced back questioningly at Caleb Jones. He did look rather grimmer than the question had merited, but even so...

'I like slightly more water in my whisky than Cal,' her father added firmly, glaring at her pointedly.

What had she said, for goodness' sake? Her father seemed almost angry, and yet she was sure her remark hadn't been that insulting. In fact, it had been tame compared to what she would have liked to have said!

'Helen!' her father prompted again, even more sharply this time.

He really was agitated; Helen frowned. Not that Caleb seemed too aware of their tension, looking very distracted.

'Sam?' she questioned her father with sudden alarm, vividly remembering the determined expression on that cherubic face two weeks ago when Sam had made his escape from his play-pen to stumble across the road in front of her car. Surely Sam hadn't made good another escape, this time with more serious consequences?

Her concern broke through Caleb's preoccupation. 'He's fine, Helen. Really,' he assured her with a strained smile. 'Actually, his grandparents are visiting him again this weekend,' he added tautly.

Then what was he doing here? The question came instantly to mind. But a single casual glance at her father's fiercely warning expression had strangulated the question un-asked in her throat. For some reason, and she would question her father on it later, he didn't want her to pursue the subject of this visit of Cal's parents to his home. There was definitely some sort of friction there, and maybe this guessed-at animosity of Cal's own parents to-wards him would give her an advantage against him she hadn't expected to find.

'I'll get your drinks,' she complied briskly. But her curiosity had been aroused now, and she would make sure she had the answer to a few questions before very long had passed.

The two men were already seated on either side of the chess-board by the time she re-turned with their drinks, and from the intent expressions on their faces, and their almost absent-minded acknowledgements of the glasses being placed beside them, she knew that they were already so engrossed by the chal-lenge ahead of them that they were barely aware of her presence.

She moved quietly across the room, picking up the book she had brought with her, to sit down in an armchair.

But she didn't find the gentle ticking of the clock, the only sound in the room other than the soft thud of the pieces being moved about the chess-board, in the least restful. The story-line that had held her attention with ease during her hours of relaxation in London now held little appeal for her, and she found her attention wandering constantly to the two men seated across the room.

Cal was concentrating as hard as her father, and yet she knew enough about the game to realise that the younger man was losing badly. She had thought the two men would be evenly matched, and yet she could see that tonight Cal was very distracted. She could also see his impatience with himself as he easily lost the first game.

Her father looked concerned, attempting a teasing smile as they set up the board for another game. 'Feel like a breather before we play again? Or a top up?' He held up their almost empty glasses.

Cal relaxed back in his chair, flexing his shoulders tiredly. 'Yes to both, thanks.' He gave a rueful smile and turned to Helen conversationally. 'Let's hope the weather stays fine for your holiday.'

She bristled resentfully; this man did have a way of saying the wrong thing. Unless it was deliberate? 'I'm not on holiday,' she snapped, feeling none of the indulgence towards him for the remark that she had felt for her father earlier.

'Helen,' her father reproved wearily. 'Stop being so touchy.' He frowned. Now is not the time, he seemed to add silently.

She frowned questioningly, but he shook his head warningly. Lord, what was so sensitive about Cal's parents visiting him? Only they weren't visiting *him*, were they? It was Sam they had obviously come to see. She really would have to talk to her father later. Perhaps, without being too nasty about it, she could point out to her father that Cal might not be quite the nice man he thought he was when his own parents treated him so suspiciously.

Whatever it was about his parents' visit that was bothering Cal, it had really got to him, and he lost the next two games of chess to her father with little resistance. He sat back with a rueful sigh. 'It's not my night tonight, I'm afraid,' he grimaced.

'Another whisky?' Helen's father prompted lightly.

Cal looked down consideringly at his empty glass. 'I don't think I'd better...' he said reluctantly, obviously in no hurry to leave.

'Coffee, then,' her father decided firmly. 'You two have a chat while I go and get it ready.'

Helen glared at him as he left the room with a mischievous wink in her direction. The old devil, he was enjoying this situation altogether too much for her liking.

'Good book?' Cal stood up, stretching stiffly.

She hadn't read a single page since she'd sat down, had spent the entire time watching the two men, fascinated by the intensity of their game! But she wasn't about to admit that! 'Not bad,' she dismissed with a shrug. 'A bit like her others.' She had read enough of the book while in London to be able to say that with complete authority. But it was a safe read, with a predictable ending, and it didn't need too much concentration to read it.

Lord, he did look tired, she realised with a frown. 'How did the interviews go?' she prompted lightly.

He brightened a little. 'Very well, actually. I have someone starting who seems very competent.'

'That will relieve some of the pressure,' she nodded.

'Let's hope so.' He still seemed distracted.

'Does Sam not get on with his grand-parents?' She frowned; all the more reason for Cal *not* to be here tonight if that was the case!

'Reasonably well,' he replied.

Then what was the problem? Because there certainly was one. 'I'm sure my father wouldn't have minded if you had missed your game of chess for one week,' Helen said softly.

'What . . .? Oh,' his brow cleared. 'No, I can assure you that I'm not necessary at the house tonight,' he added grimly.

He *didn't* get on with Sam's grandparents. Curiouser and curiouser—as the saying went. She could hardly wait to talk to her father alone.

But the two men seemed in no hurry to bring the evening to a close, relaxing back in a couple of armchairs to talk lightly as they enjoyed their coffee.

Helen studied Caleb Jones again, wondering at her earlier reaction to him. Oh, he was handsome enough, rakishly so, but that very fact should have been enough to repulse her; she had learnt the hard way that dangerously attractive men were selfishly obsessed with having life their own way. Caleb Jones had done little, so far, to disabuse her of that belief!

Besides, she had more sense than to ever let personal feelings towards a man interfere with her life a second time!

She stood up determinedly. 'I think I'd better go to bed.'

Caleb frowned, glancing down at his watch. 'I suppose I'd better be on my way.' But he didn't sound in the least anxious to go.

'There's no need to do that just because I'm going to bed,' Helen dismissed briskly. 'Stay and have another drink with my father.'

Caleb stood up too. 'I'm sure I'll see you again soon.'

So was she, but she had accepted that such meetings were unavoidable before she came down here!

He chuckled softly at the revealing expression on her face. 'Your enthusiasm for that idea is overwhelming!'

She blushed at the amused sarcasm in his voice, looking reluctantly at her father, expecting censure in his face but finding the other man's humour reflected there. The *two* of them were actually enjoying her discomfort now!

'Goodnight, Mr Jones,' she said with as much dignity as she could muster. 'Daddy,' she kissed him with a warmth that was accompanied by a saccharine-sweet smile, the look in her eyes promising further comment on his behaviour when they were alone.

Whether Caleb took up her suggestion or not, he stayed downstairs talking with her father for at least another half-hour after she had gone up to her bedroom. She became aware of the sound of his car leaving as she came through from taking her shower, strolling over to the window to watch his tail-lights disappearing in the direction of the main house, absently drying her hair with a towel as she wondered what sort of reception awaited him. It was his home, and yet she knew it was the last place he wanted to be tonight.

Her father was still seated in the lounge when she got downstairs, his expression pensive, although he brightened somewhat as she came into the room.

'I thought you would have been asleep long ago,' he said with a smile.

She shrugged. 'I needed a shower. And I thought perhaps Caleb wanted to talk to you alone for a while,' she added.

Her father grimaced. 'It isn't an easy situation for him.'

'But he must have realised that when he first took Sam on.' She frowned. 'And he could make things a lot easier for himself if he employed a nanny to help out.'

'Oh, it isn't caring for Sam that's the problem,' her father dismissed impatiently.

Helen looked at him questioningly, but he seemed lost in his own thoughts, and after a couple of minutes' silence from him she realised he wasn't about to explain himself.

'Then what is?' she prompted softly, her eyes narrowed thoughtfully.

'Sam's grandparents,' he said heavily.

The subject she had been longing to get back to all evening!

'What about them?' she voiced as casually as she was able.

'Oh, they mean well, I suppose,' her father sighed. 'And I'm sure they love Sam and want what's best for him, but . . .' He trailed off with a sigh.

'But?' she said gently.

'Sam loves Cal very much; they're great together.' He frowned.

'And?' Helen looked at him expectantly.

Her father stood up, moving to pour himself a cup of what must be lukewarm coffee by now. 'It's always a messy business when children are involved in a custody wrangle.' He shook his head.

'Cal's *own* parents are fighting him for the custody of Sam?' she gasped. Lord, this was worse than she had thought! Cal must have done something really outrageous for his own parents to think him unsuitable to bring Sam up. She couldn't even begin to guess what it might have been.

'Of course not,' her father denied censoriously.

'But——'

'The grandparents visiting Sam at the moment are the parents of Sam's mother,' her father said impatiently, as if that explained everything.

And maybe it did to a certain extent, although certainly not completely. Sam's father must obviously have been Cal's brother, but that didn't tell her why the baby's maternal grandparents were so against Cal's having custody of him.

Her father gave an irritated sigh. 'When Sam's parents were killed in a car accident both Cal and Susan's parents were left as guardians of the baby, with Cal having actual custody of him.'

'That seems clear enough.' Helen nodded slowly.

'Possibly,' her father acknowledged tersely. 'At least, you would think it was. But the grandparents were never happy about the situation, claiming that it would be best for Sam to grow up in a normal family atmosphere—that is with both a man and a woman to care for him. Namely themselves,' he added grimly. 'In the last few months they have been putting great pressure on Cal to let them have Sam.'

'And he doesn't agree?' Helen said softly.

'Well of course he doesn't!' her father snapped.

Helen shrugged. 'But maybe they do have a point, maybe Sam would be better off with them——'

'You know something, Helen,' her father cut in with cold anger, 'I sometimes wonder if you can possibly be my daughter after all.' He turned and strode furiously from the room.

Helen looked after him with dismay; her father had never spoken to her with that flat disappointment in his voice before.

CHAPTER FIVE

DAMN Caleb Jones and the trouble he was
causing Helen!

By the time morning came, following that
disagreement with her father over the custody
of Sam, Helen had decided it was all Caleb
Jones's fault. If he weren't their intrusive
neighbour now, none of last night's conversation would have taken place. Certainly she
and her father would never have argued in that
way.

She knew her father was still displeased with
her when she came downstairs to find a brief
note in the kitchen from him telling her he had
gone to the golf-course for the day. Normally
he would have asked her to go with him, but
obviously he was still so disgusted with her that
he didn't even want to be in her company.

She still couldn't see what was so wrong
about her comment that perhaps Sam would
be better off with his grandparents. Obviously
Cal was a friend of her father's, and his loyalty
lay with the other man, but surely Sam's
grandparents couldn't be such ogres that they
shouldn't be considered even more suitable as

stand-in parents for Sam rather than a man on his own. Especially when that man was as rakishly good-looking as Cal Jones was; poor Sam could live the rest of his life having a succession of 'aunties'!

Nevertheless, she could understand her father's sympathy with the other man's feelings, and cursed herself for being so insensitive. Hopefully her father would have mellowed after a day playing golf, and would be willing to accept her apology. Although she wouldn't count on it; her father could be more stubborn than her on occasion. That was where she had got that stubborn streak from in the first place!

As an added apology Helen prepared a curry ready for their dinner later in the day, knowing it was one of her father's favourite meals, but at the same time one he very rarely bothered to make just for himself. He would know the meal was something of a peace-offering, but that didn't matter.

The curry was bubbling away nicely when the telephone rang, and she groaned as she moved to answer it; it was just like her father to realise what she would do and be ringing to tell her he was out to dinner!

'Good morning, Helen,' Cal Jones's deeply attractive voice greeted confidently. 'Could I speak to your father, please?'

Helen frowned her agitation with having to talk to this man who was starting to become a permanent thorn in her side. 'I'm afraid he isn't here,' she said with a certain amount of satisfaction.

'Oh, damn,' she heard him mutter distractedly.

'Is there something wrong?' Helen couldn't help her curiosity.

'No, not really—— Hell, yes,' he amended with a groan. 'I'm determined to have this thing out with Sam's grandparents once and for all, and I didn't want Sam around while we did it. He's very sensitive to the atmosphere which exists between the three of us, which was another reason I decided to make myself scarce last night,' he added grimly, and Helen could clearly picture the worry on that handsome face. 'He and your father get on really well together, and I was going to ask David if he would mind having Sam for the afternoon.'

'I'll have him,' Helen heard herself say, instantly wanting to retract the statement, opening her mouth to do so. But the words wouldn't come, her tongue seeming to be stuck to the roof of her mouth.

The last thing she wanted was to be in the company of that mischievously beautiful child for any length of time. But the words of denial still wouldn't come, even though she could feel her own panic rising within her.

'I couldn't put on you like that.' Cal's frown could be heard in his voice.

Now was the time to agree with him, to give the impression her offer had only been made out of politeness!

But the words seemed to be stuck in her throat. 'You wouldn't be putting on me,' she told him briskly, all the time her brain screaming at her to agree with him, anything to keep her from having to spend time with the baby. 'I have the afternoon free anyway,' she heard herself add persuasively.

'If you're sure...?'

Of course she wasn't sure; she didn't *want* to look after Sam!

'I'm sure,' she said firmly. 'I'll come over and get him around two o'clock, if that's OK?'

'I could drive him over for you,' Cal offered, still sounding distracted.

'No, I'll come and pick him up, I might take him shopping straight after that.' What on earth was she doing? It was bad enough that she had offered to look after Sam at all, but she didn't have to add to the mistake by appearing in public with a baby that would be taken as her own as she walked along with him in his pushchair!

'OK, two o'clock, then. I really do appreciate this, Helen,' Cal added warmly.

She didn't want his gratitude, for goodness' sake—didn't want to be looking after Sam at all.

She was shaking as she replaced the telephone after saying goodbye to Cal. Sam to look after all afternoon... What had she been thinking of? She hadn't been thinking at all! At least, nothing that had passed from her brain to her tongue.

What was she going to do with a year-old baby for the afternoon?

Oh, this was ridiculous; she should just ring Cal back and tell him she had made a mistake, that she had something else to do this afternoon after all. But pride wouldn't let her do that, to telephone Cal and give the impression she was incapable of looking after Sam. Even if, emotionally, that was just how she felt.

She was too upset to eat any lunch, had almost burnt the curry by leaving it on too high a heat rather than letting the flavour be enhanced by leaving it to gently simmer, and she left the house to collect Sam with the feeling of a heavy weight having been put on her shoulders.

Her trepidation grew as she drove nearer to the manor house, vaguely noticing the improvements Cal had made to the garden since he had taken over the estate, her feet crunching on the gravel as she got out of the car.

'Helen!'

She turned guiltily, having almost given in to the temptation to get back in her car and drive off again, afraid that emotion might show in her face as she turned to look at Cal striding across the lawn towards her, Sam held in his arms.

She was struck once again by the likeness between the two of them, the same coal-black hair, the same navy-blue eyes, even their smiles similar as Sam laughed up into his uncle's face, his eyes glowing with good health—and mischief. He wasn't the sort of little boy who would ever be cowed by anything, completely happy in his environment. Which somehow made it all the more poignant that he didn't have his parents to share in his happiness. What a lot of pleasure this little boy would have brought into his parents' lives; she could see why Cal was loath to part with him. But at the same time, whatever decisions were made had to be in Sam's favour, and no one else's. And she was sure Cal was all too aware of that, which might, or might not, explain his strain over the situation.

'Two o'clock, as requested,' she said in a stilted voice.

Cal looked at her searchingly. 'You're sure you want to do this? Sam is usually good, but nevertheless it's an imposition,' he grimaced.

She was no more sure now than she had been this morning when she had so recklessly agreed to take care of Sam, but it was far too late to change her mind now.

'I have to go into town shopping anyway,' she dismissed carelessly—hoping *her own* strain wasn't too obvious. 'I can do that just as easily with Sam as without him.' Although she very much doubted that was true—a pushchair was an encumbrance few mothers managed to overcome!

'Shide, Unc Cal,' Sam cried excitedly.

'When you get back,' Cal told him indulgently. 'We were playing on the slide beside the house when you arrived,' he explained to Helen.

'Shide gen, Unc Cal,' Sam repeated mutinously.

'I'll take him back on the slide while you get his pushchair—and anything else you think I might need this afternoon,' Helen added heavily, holding out her arms for Sam. To her surprise he came to her without hesitation.

Cal gave a rueful smile. 'I hate to sound depressing, but he'll go to anyone who will take him on the slide!'

'Thanks!' she grimaced, turning to walk towards the side of the house.

Sam felt just as soft and cuddly as the last time she had held him, with that uniquely baby smell that was so unmistakable.

It was impossible not to join in his joy as he came down the tiny slide that had been erected in part of the garden obviously fenced off just for Sam's use, a sand-pit and small swing also available for his pleasure, although the slide was obviously his favourite as he went down it time and time again, with help from her to get up the two steps to the top of the slide.

'Enjoying yourself, Sam?'

Helen turned with widened eyes, the male voice not a familiar one to her, although it was obvious as she looked at the middle-aged couple who had come to stand outside the fenced-off area that this must be Sam's grandparents. Sam bore no likeness to either the short balding man or the taller blonde-haired woman, but nevertheless Helen didn't think they could be anyone else.

'I don't think he should be on that slide, Henry,' the woman said waspishly. 'He could fall and hurt himself.'

The likelihood of Sam's doing that seemed very remote to Helen, the slide only a couple of feet high, with the soft landing of lush grass if he should topple over. Although with someone having to help him up the steps in the first place this seemed highly unlikely at all.

'I doubt that, dear,' the man replied drily, giving Helen a friendly smile. 'I'm sorry, we haven't introduced ourselves. I'm Henry Carter, and this is my wife, Enid. We're Sam's grandparents.'

'I'm Helen Foster, a—a friend of Cal's.' She had been going to say 'a neighbour' of Cal's, but considering she was taking this couple's grandson off for the afternoon she thought she ought to at least be a friend of the family!

'Are you——?'

'Enid, Henry, I wondered where you had got to!' Cal strode across the lawn towards them all, his voice light, although his tone was belied by the worried expression in his eyes as he looked at them searchingly. 'Have you all introduced yourselves?' He arched questioning brows as he joined them.

'Yes, thank you.' Enid Carter spoke tartly, her back ramrod straight. 'Sam, come down off that slide at once,' she instructed the little boy as Helen helped him up the steps once again.

Sam hesitated for a moment, his expression one of confusion, before his eyes filled up with tears and he held out his arms towards Helen to be picked up, burying his face in her neck to hide the tears, his little body shaking with the emotion.

Helen looked at Cal for support, not in any position to deal with the older woman herself, but feeling the injustice of the instruction on Sam's behalf. There was sensible protection of a small child, and *over*-protection, and it seemed to her that Enid Carter was indulging in the latter. But that wasn't for her to say so.

Cal looked at Helen, speaking volumes with his eyes. 'I've put the pushchair and a few of Sam's favourite toys next to your car,' he told her softly, at the same time his expression pleading for her understanding of the situation.

And in a small way she was starting to understand his dilemma; Enid Carter could, if allowed to dominate Sam on a permanent basis, dampen all the spirit that made him such an enchanting child. Although she could be misjudging the other woman, Helen reproved herself; concern for the child's well-being had to be a good thing. And Sam's grandmother might just be over-protective of him because she had so recently lost her daughter. Who was she, Helen, to judge the other woman on such short acquaintance? Besides, from the few occasions she had had to see Sam with Cal Jones she didn't have any reason to suppose he was any better for the child.

But she took his hint for her to leave with Sam, holding the little boy tightly against her, an unwanted feeling of compassion for the dilemma of his future making her want to take him right away from the conflict.

'Do you like the zoo, Sam?' she asked him softly as she left his play area, not sparing another glance for the other adults present. They were old enough to sort out their own problems; Sam was the one who was important now. She just hoped they resolved this problem quickly, and that the conflict stopped, although from the tight-lipped expression on Enid Carter's face she thought it would take a lot for her to do that. Possibly only complete victory on her part.

Sam's face came out of her neck at the word 'zoo', his eyes glowing. 'Anmals?' he said hopefully.

Lord, he was adorable, she acknowledged achingly. By the end of this afternoon she was going to be his slave for life; she had already forgone the thought of shopping in the hope of pleasing him!

He seemed totally happy going out with her in the car, his seat, and him, easily strapped into the back seat, his gaze flashing everywhere as he looked about them interestedly. It took all of Helen's concentration to keep her attention on the road in front of them and not keep indulging in glances at Sam in her driving mirror.

Away from a situation that was obviously causing him unhappiness, Sam blossomed, completely forgetting the few words he did know as he talked to each animal at the zoo in turn in his baby gibberish. Not that the animals seemed to mind, sensing from the tone of his voice the sheer joy he felt in looking at them, several of the monkeys coming to the sides of their penned area to talk gibberish back to him!

It was an afternoon of complete pleasure for Helen. Sam needed a sharp eye kept on him at all times, but was still a delight to be with. He was completely without guile, stubborn but not deliberately wilful.

And by the end of the afternoon in his company Helen could more than understand why it was that Cal was so reluctant to part with him. Even if it was to the child's advantage. But that was still debatable, in the face of Enid Carter's over-protective manner. Helen could just imagine the other woman being completely horrified at the thought of Sam even being near the 'smelly animals', as she was sure the other woman would consider them.

Although that was jumping to conclusions, she mentally rebuked herself. But, sadly, she had a feeling that was exactly the way Enid Carter would feel.

'Unc Cal?' Sam said hopefully as Helen belted him back into the car for their homeward journey.

'Unc Cal.' She nodded, knowing the desire to see his uncle again was no reflection on the time they had just spent together; Sam had enjoyed himself at the zoo, of that she had no doubt. That he might have enjoyed it more if his uncle had been present was possible, but on the whole she would say it had been a successful afternoon.

But she could feel her own tension grow as they approached the estate; what if Cal and the Carters were still arguing?

Well, she would just have to take Sam home with her for a while, she decided firmly. Arguments of that kind were not suitable for a small child to hear; even one as young as Sam would pick up the tension in the atmosphere.

All seemed quiet when she and Sam were let into the house some time later by the young maid, although from the little she had come to know of Cal during their short acquaintance she didn't think he was the type to scream and shout to achieve putting over his point anyway.

'Mr Jones and his guests are in the sitting-room,' the maid informed her before quietly disappearing into the depths of the house.

It was the first time Helen had been into the house since Cal Jones had taken it over, and she had to admit, even if a little reluctantly, that the changes he had made were for the better. The house, which had once seemed so cold and formal, was now warm and welcoming, with an untidy elegance that allowed for the children's toys scattered about the entrance hall, obviously left there earlier by Sam, a Sam who now squirmed in her arms to be let down to play with them again.

Helen put him down, after first checking that there was no way the little boy could make an escape up the wide staircase that led up to the wide open gallery before leading to the many bedrooms. A specially built gate, little-finger-proof, had been put in at the bottom of the stairs to achieve avoiding just such an occurrence.

To give Cal Jones his due, she allowed grudgingly, he had done everything that he could to assure the safety of the adorable child in his care.

She left Sam playing on the carpet with a fire-engine and several large cars, knocking softly on the door of the room the maid had pointed out as the room Cal occupied with his guests, choosing to announce her own presence.

She was completely unprepared for the door being wrenched open mid-knock as Enid Carter stormed out of the room! The other woman

had two red spots of anger on her cheeks, her
pale blue eyes blazing with unsuppressed fury.

She turned angrily on Helen as she saw her
standing there. 'It's only natural that I should
want my grandson with me!'

'Er—well—yes . . .' Helen answered lamely,
completely taken aback by the attack.

'Enid——'

'Be quiet, Henry,' his wife snapped harshly,
turning to Cal with flashing eyes. 'I don't care
how far you're prepared to go in your effort at
respectability, I won't rest until I have Sam
living with me!'

'Enid, we keep going round and round this
situation until I start to feel giddy,' Cal answered wearily, obviously having spent most of
his afternoon going over the same arguments—and getting absolutely nowhere.

Helen felt embarrassed at being caught in the
middle of it all, had felt sure this conversation
would have been over long ago, otherwise she
wouldn't have brought Sam back when she had.

'Graham and Susan wanted Sam to live with
me,' Cal continued gently. 'Doesn't that count
for anything?' he reasoned softly.

'When Graham and Susan made that con-
dition they hardly thought the two of them
would be dead within a year,' Enid Carter
snapped. 'It's only natural for them to have
assumed that Henry and I would either be al-

ready dead or at least far too old to take on the care of a child if the situation had arisen that both of *them* would be dead. That only left them with the one choice, unsuitable as that one is,' she added coldly.

Helen heard Cal's angry intake of breath, wishing herself anywhere but in the midst of this very private conversation. She waited anxiously for Cal's explosion, eyeing him nervously.

'Enid, I've done everything within my power to make a stable life for Sam,' Cal finally said quietly, his own anger firmly under control, although it hadn't been easy for him to achieve, by the impatient fury in his eyes. 'No one, not even you,' he assured the older woman firmly, 'could have done more for him than I have.' He looked at her challengingly, although the stress of the last few hours was starting to show in the strain about his eyes and mouth and the slight pallor to his skin.

'Money can achieve a lot,' Enid Carter acknowledged bitterly. 'But then you and your brother have always been aware of that!'

Cal's mouth tightened. 'I don't think bringing the past into this is going to help the situation in the——'

'*Help* the situation?' the middle-aged woman echoed shrilly. 'If your brother hadn't dazzled my daughter with his wealth and charm none of this would have happened in the first place, because Susan would never have been married to him!' she said accusingly. 'Susan was engaged to a *nice* young man when your brother forced his way into her life——'

'Susan and Graham loved each other very much,' Cal began with careful deliberation, as if controlling his anger with extreme difficulty now.

As, indeed, Helen could quite believe he was! Enid Carter obviously had a lot of old bitterness that still pained her deeply, and although some of the accusations she was levelling at Cal, the ones about money in particular, weren't so different from what Helen herself had been saying, she still wished herself anywhere but witnessing this highly personal conversation.

'Susan was overwhelmed by the attentions of a rich and experienced man,' her mother said with contempt for the man who had become her son-in-law.

'Enid,' her husband began reasoningly.

'You and your brother believe you can buy anything.' She completely ignored the interruption. 'Even women.' She looked accusingly at Helen now.

Helen's eyes widened at this fresh attack on her, more personal this time.

'Enid, I believe that's enough,' Cal told her with quiet intensity. 'Attacks on me are one thing, but I won't have Helen involved in this.'

The older woman's mouth twisted disdainfully. 'I would say she is already very much involved,' she snapped. 'The two of you are—*friends*, didn't you say?' She looked challengingly at Helen.

Hot colour flooded her cheeks. 'Yes, I did, But——'

'*Good* friends, I would say,' the other woman scorned.

'Enid!' Cal rasped harshly. 'Our relationship isn't in the least like the one you are implying!'

Enid Carter recoiled as if he had struck her. 'You don't mean the two of you are getting *married*?' she gasped. 'Don't you believe that is going a little too far in your bid for respectability?' she added accusingly.

Now it was Helen's turn to gasp; she had gone from offering, recklessly, to help Cal out with Sam for the afternoon, to bluntly being accused of marrying Cal for his money. *Marrying* the man? The idea was ludicrous. Ridiculous. Laughable. Although *nothing* about this conversation was really funny.

'Enid,' Cal spoke softly, but the cold fury was there none the less, 'Helen is a friend who has very kindly helped me out today. I will not have her insulted, by you or anyone else.'

Helen looked at him. After the things *she* had accused him of, he could still champion her in this way? Although, she had to admit, their own difference of opinion had nothing to do with this situation.

'If she marries you she will have my *pity*, not my insults,' Enid Carter scorned. 'Come along, Henry,' she instructed arrogantly. 'I don't think there is anything to be gained by continuing this conversation.' She walked out of the room without waiting to see if her husband complied with her order, seeming to know that he would do so without her having to repeat it a second time.

And who could blame the poor man? Helen mentally sympathised; Enid Carter in full flow was a force to be reckoned with. Although she had to admit that Cal had more than held his own against the other woman.

Henry Carter made a move towards the door, and hesitated, before turning back to the two of them. 'I really am sorry about this.' He shook his head worriedly. 'I know you're only doing what you think is best, Cal.' He gave a helpless shrug.

Cal gave a wry grimace. 'Try and convince Enid of that, will you?'

The other man sighed. 'Susan was our only child,' he answered, as if that explained everything.

And perhaps it did. Sam was all this couple had left of their daughter. Although Helen didn't think Cal had much family to talk of either, so perhaps the same was true for him about his brother. It really was a difficult situation, for all concerned.

But at the end of the day it was really Sam's welfare they all had to think of, and, much as Helen found it hard to admit, if she were truthful, and from what she had seen today, Cal Jones was the right person to bring Sam up. Sadly, she was sure Henry Carter knew that too, although his loyalty obviously had to remain with his wife. Perhaps even Enid Carter knew the truth of that too, and that was why her reaction against it was so strong. After all, the other woman was in her sixties, and the responsibility of taking on a child of Sam's age at this stage in her life would be a great one. Guilt could be as much of an incentive to anger as anything else.

And Helen should know. It was her own guilt at not being with her father enough over the last seven months to know what was going on in his life that had made her so angry with herself the last couple of weeks.

But whatever the reason for Enid Carter's fury it was very real none the less, and could have serious consequences for all concerned.

'I know.' Cal squeezed the other man's arm reassuringly. 'But we all want what's best for Sam, don't we?'

The older man sighed at the truth of that. 'I'll try and talk Enid into seeing sense,' he offered, but his weary expression didn't hold out much hope of his doing that. He turned to Helen. 'I'm sorry you had to get caught up in this, Miss Foster.' He shook his head at the hopelessness of the situation.

'That's all right.' Helen gave him a reassuring smile, knowing her involvement had been purely incidental; anyone walking in on that fraught situation would have been likely to have been drawn into it, no matter how much they might have wished they wouldn't be.

He turned back to Cal once more. 'I really am sorry.' His expression became even more worried as he followed his wife out of the room.

Cal let out a deep sigh in an effort to relieve some of his tension, his hand shaking slightly as he ran it through his already tousled hair, as if it was far from the first time he had made the action this afternoon.

Helen could only guess at the tension of the conversation before she had come back, although if it had been anything like what she *had* heard it was enough to make Cal want to pull his hair out, not just tousle it!

'I can see now why you wanted Sam away from the house this afternoon,' she said ruefully, giving a quick glance out into the entrance hall to check that he was still playing with his toys. The events of the last half-hour had completely gone over his tiny little head as he concentrated on putting out imaginary fires in the cars.

Cal shook his head wearily. 'This battle has been going on for months now, and quite honestly I'm coming to the end of my patience.'

'It can't be good for Sam,' she sympathised softly.

He sighed. 'For the main part I've tried to keep him away from it, but children his age are quick to pick up tension, and that's the least of my emotions when Enid chooses to descend on us at the weekends!'

If they had this battle every weekend she wasn't surprised. No wonder he felt the need to escape from his own home on Friday evenings to enjoy the lull of those few hours spent in relaxation with her father before the storm of the weekend began!

'I'm sorry you were drawn into it the way you were.' He looked at her anxiously.

'It wasn't your fault,' she shrugged, although her cheeks burnt from the accusations the other woman had made concerning the two of them.

And how would she have felt about the conversation if she really were a special friend of Cal's? It would have been devastating to have such remarks made about their relationship.

'The really sad part of all this is that Enid knows how much Graham loved Susan, he just wasn't her idea of a son-in-law,' he added ruefully. 'That "nice" young man Enid referred to whom Susan was going to marry was the type that Enid would have been able to dominate, and so not really lose her influence over Susan.' He shook his head. 'Marrying Graham against her mother's wishes was the one and only open act of defiance that Susan ever committed. And Enid never let her forget it,' he said grimly.

Or her dislike of the man her daughter had married, if her comments a few minutes ago were anything to go by! It was far from the ideal way to begin a marriage.

'I say "open" act of defiance because if Enid only knew...' Cal gave a pained groan.

'Yes?' Helen couldn't help prompting, felt as if she had just read a book only to get to the last page and find it was missing. As indeed she now felt it was. And it was in Cal's possession.

He drew in a ragged breath, visibly shaken now by the scene that had just transpired. 'I wish Enid would just let up on the pressure, because one of these days I'm not going to be able to restrain myself... And if that happens I'm going to do something unforgivable.' He shook his head again.

She could see his anguish at the very idea of it, could only guess at the effort it cost him to restrain himself from dealing with Enid Carter once and for all.

Cal looked at her with pained eyes. 'I'm not a deliberately cruel man.' His mouth twisted ruefully. 'No matter what you might think to the contrary...'

If she was honest she didn't really know what she thought any more. She hated it when the so-called heroines of television programmes came out with that hackneyed old line 'I'm so confused', but at this moment that was exactly what she was! Cal's dealings with her father over Cherry Trees seemed underhand to her, and yet his control with Enid Carter, gentleness almost, in the face of constant insults, spoke of a completely different sort of man from the one she had imagined him to be.

She put her hand on his arm, her eyes widening in alarm when he turned to her with a groan, gathering her into his arms to bury his face against her throat.

Her alarm turned to panic as she realised how right it felt to be held against him like this, Enid

Carter and the previous tension forgotten as she raised her face to Cal's.

Dark blue eyes devoured the paleness of her face before he slowly lowered his head and claimed her lips with his own. Liquid warmth flowed through her veins as his mouth moved sensuously against hers, his hands cupping her face now as he held her lips up for the slow, searching kiss that made her legs tremble and her body shake. His shoulders felt muscled beneath her supporting hands, his body hard against hers, as the kiss went on and on, searching and tormenting at the same time, Helen's whole body on fire for a deepening of the caress.

'Sam kiss.'

Helen pulled back in horror to look down at the little boy pulling on her skirt for attention. He needn't worry, he had her full attention— she dared not even look at Cal!

CHAPTER SIX

'CAL'S on the phone. For you,' her father added softly.

Helen's pulse jumped tensely at the mention of the other man's name, but she could feel it beating a nervous tattoo at her temple when her father told her the call from him was for her.

She stood up disjointedly, unable to stand her father's knowing gaze a moment longer. 'He probably just wants to thank me again for taking Sam out for him yesterday afternoon,' she said sharply, smoothing her skirt agitatedly.

Her father watched the movement with an amused twist to his lips. 'Yes, you're probably right,' he replied without sincerity, his eyes twinkling with merry humour.

Not that Helen could altogether blame him. By the time she had arrived home yesterday evening her nerves hadn't settled down at all after that unexpected kiss from Cal and its abrupt, and embarrassing, ending, and she had walked in to find her father had got home before her. Her flushed cheeks and over-bright eyes could have been attributed to anger or inner turmoil, and she had known within a few minutes that her father had drawn the right conclusion. He had been eyeing her with that knowing amusement ever since!

It had been embarrassing enough to have Sam witness that kiss between his uncle and herself. She had hastily pulled out of Cal's arms, keeping her face averted from his searching gaze as she'd bent down to talk to the little boy. By the time she had stood up again she had been slightly more under control, although her gaze still hadn't quite been able to meet Cal's as she'd made her excuses to leave.

Her agitation had returned in full force when he had accompanied her to the door to take her hand in his. She had been unable to do anything else but look at him then, and the tenderness in his eyes had almost been her undoing, her natural instinct being to move back into the warm security of his arms.

But she had resisted the temptation, snatching her hand out of his as she had mumbled her goodbyes and fled out of the house into the sunshine.

She still didn't quite know what had happened between them yesterday. The shadows under her eyes were evidence of the sleepless night she had spent wondering how one moment she could have been talking to Cal quite sensibly and the next moment be in his arms returning his kisses. It was so completely out of character for her, and the knowledge of how desperately she had wanted the kisses to continue terrified the life out of her.

What on earth could he want to talk to her about now?

Maybe she was right, maybe he did just want to thank her again for taking Sam yesterday. Although somehow she doubted it; she knew *he* hadn't wanted the kisses to stop yesterday either!

'Yes?' Her voice was restrained, and yet slightly breathless, a churning sensation in her stomach as she clutched the receiver in her hand.

'Helen.'

Just the sound of her name on his lips was enough to tell her that no time might have elapsed since she had been in his arms, that the distance between them didn't exist, that the telephone was no barrier to the desire he still felt for her!

She moistened her lips with the tip of her tongue, almost able to taste him there. This was madness, a mere flight of the senses, and yet it was real, so very real.

'I have to see you——'

'No!' she protested sharply, taking a calming breath, knowing she was over-reacting, clearly revealing her confusion over the situation, 'I don't think that would be a good idea,' she amended distantly.

There was silence for several long seconds, and when Cal spoke again it was in a briskly businesslike tone, all huskiness gone from his voice. 'I'd like to take you out to dinner as a thank-you for——'

'I would rather not,' she cut in abruptly. 'I— I'm busy,' she added shortly.

'You don't know which evening I was asking you yet,' Cal returned a little mockingly.

Fool, she chastised herself. What had happened to the cool-headed, sensible person she usually was? If she had been that person yesterday, none of this conversation would be taking place!

'I'm here to spend time with my father,' she told him tartly.

'I'm sure David can spare your company for one night,' he drawled derisively.

She was sure he could too, if it was to spend time with Cal Jones. But she had no intention of telling her father of the invitation.

'Tomorrow night will be fine,' David Foster remarked behind her.

Helen spun round, glaring at her father accusingly for listening in on her side of the telephone conversation, at least.

'Did David say tomorrow night?' Cal prompted with mocking humour.

She gave her father one last glare of censure before pointedly turning her back on him. 'What my father says really has nothing to do with it——'

'But a few minutes ago you said that it did,' Cal reminded teasingly.

'I was trying to refuse you politely!' she snapped impatiently. Really, these two were like a comedy act, and she was their 'straight man'! She would swear Cal had put her father up to this, if she didn't know better; her father needed no encouragement to be interfering where he thought it was for her own good. But he couldn't possibly know how fraught with possibilities her seeing Cal Jones could be.

'Try impolitely,' Cal drawled challengingly. 'Otherwise I might keep asking you.'

'I don't want to have dinner with you, tomorrow or any other night,' she said irritably.

'I'm sure you can do better than that, Helen,' he mocked.

'Surely I was explicit enough?' Her impatience deepened.

'Explicit, yes,' he acknowledged. 'But your refusal leaves a little room for doubt.'

'What doubt?' she said incredulously. 'Surely a refusal is a refusal, no matter how it's put?'

' "You lousy swine" on the end of it might be more convincing,' Cal teased.

She wasn't sure she thought of him as a 'lousy swine' any more. In fact, she had been trying not to think of him at all today, although it had been proving a little difficult.

'Oh, go on, Helen,' her father cajoled. 'Say yes to the man.'

She wasn't sure what she was saying yes to, that was the trouble! Her reasons for being wary of Cal Jones seemed to have changed drastically during the last twenty-four hours.

Which was ridiculous. She wasn't frightened of any man, especially the sort of man she believed Cal Jones to be. She completely ignored that nagging little voice at the back of her mind that told her she wasn't sure about *that* any more either. 'All right,' she sighed. 'Dinner tomorrow. But on the strict understanding it's only as a thank-you for taking Sam out,' she warned.

'As if I would think it was for anything else,' Cal drawled.

'As if,' her father murmured tauntingly very close to her ear.

Helen rounded on him. 'Will you just go away?' She glared at him.

'If you insist,' Cal drawled. 'But——'

'Not you,' she told him impatiently, furious with her father. But he just grinned back at

NO COST! NO OBLIGATION TO BUY!
NO PURCHASE NECESSARY!

PLAY "LUCKY 7"
AND GET AS MANY AS SIX FREE GIFTS...

HOW TO PLAY:

1. With a coin, carefully scratch off the silver box at the right. This makes you eligible to receive two or more free books, and possibly other gifts, depending on what is revealed beneath the scratch-off area.

2. You'll receive brand-new Harlequin Presents® novels. When you return this card, we'll send you the books and gifts you qualify for *absolutely free!*

3. If we don't hear from you, every month, we'll send you 6 additional novels to read and enjoy. You can return them and owe nothing but if you decide to keep them, you'll pay only $2.49* per book, a saving of 40¢ each off the cover price plus only 69¢ delivery for the entire shipment!

4. When you join the Harlequin Reader Service®, you'll get our subscribers'-only newsletter, as well as additional free gifts from time to time just for being a subscriber.

5. You must be completely satisfied. You may cancel at any time simply by sending us a note or a shipping statement marked ''cancel'' or by returning any shipment to us at our cost.

This lovely heart-shaped box is richly detailed with cut-glass decorations, perfect for holding a precious memento or keepsake—and it's yours absolutely free when you accept our no-risk offer.

PLAY "LUCKY 7"

**Just scratch off the silver box with a coin.
Then check below to see which gifts you get.**

YES! I have scratched off the silver box. Please send me all the gifts for which I qualify. I understand I am under no obligation to purchase any books, as explained on the opposite page.

306 CIH AEMC
(C-H-P-05/92)

NAME	
ADDRESS	APT
CITY PROVINCE	POSTAL CODE

7 7 7	WORTH FOUR FREE BOOKS, FREE HEART-SHAPED GLASS BOX AND MYSTERY BONUS
🍒 🍒 🍒	WORTH FOUR FREE BOOKS AND MYSTERY BONUS
● ● ●	WORTH THREE FREE BOOKS
🔔 🔔 🍒	WORTH TWO FREE BOOKS

Business Reply Mail

No Postage Stamp
Necessary if Mailed
in Canada

Postage will be paid by

HARLEQUIN READER SERVICE
PO BOX 609
FORT ERIE, ONT.
L2A 9Z9

her, unrepentant. 'I was talking to my father,' she crossly explained to Cal. 'He seems to have forgotten that it's rude to listen in on other people's conversations,' she added pointedly, still glaring warningly at her father as he made no effort to leave her in privacy.

'It's my house,' he said blandly.

'But my call—— Oh, damn,' she swore as she realised Cal was still listening in on this exchange, almost able to picture his amusement—at her expense. 'I'll see you tomorrow,' she told him abruptly, ringing off to look at her father in challenging reproval.

He didn't look in the least concerned by her anger. 'I wonder where he'll take you,' he mused thoughtfully.

'None of your business.' She gave an irritated sigh. 'I didn't want to go in the first place!'

'That was obvious,' he grimaced.

'Then why did you——? Oh, never mind,' she dismissed impatiently. 'I'll go and finish cooking lunch.' She went off to the kitchen before her father could say any more.

Dinner with Cal Jones tomorrow night.

How did she get herself into these situations? The answer to that was all too obvious; her father was the main reason she had helped Cal out with Sam yesterday afternoon, and he was also the reason she had been press-ganged into having dinner with the other man to-morrow evening. If her father hadn't joined in the conversation there was no way she would have allowed herself to be talked into agreeing to the invitation.

She didn't want to spend an evening alone with Cal Jones.

She hadn't been this affected by a man since—well, since Daniel.

She hated to admit it, but being in Cal Jones's arms had frightened her in a way being with Daniel never had. Because she had ached with wanting more than just being in his arms.

And she was terrified of that happening again.

This attraction she felt for Cal made her feel out of control, and it wasn't a feeling she was at all comfortable with. She had survived her years in London by being completely in control; a few days back here and her life was in turmoil. And she had a feeling it was going to get worse rather than better.

The rest of the day was spent with her suffering the smug expression of her father every time she dared a glance at him, his anger with her on Friday night completely forgotten in the face of this new development.

He might well look pleased with himself; he couldn't have been happier if he had arranged the whole thing himself!

*   *   *

'Do you want to order now or have a drink first?' Cal looked at her enquiringly.

She wanted to get the evening over with as soon as possible!

Her father's knowing looks as she had joined the two men in the lounge earlier had been enough to turn her tension into teeth-grating anger.

She had dressed for the evening ahead with great care, the deep green dress fitted at the bodice but flowing silkily about her long legs, its style smart rather than provocative. Her hair she had compromised on, securing it back on either side from her face with two ornate combs, but leaving it flowing loosely down her spine. Her appearance wasn't severe enough to incur her father's critisism, but it was enough for her to feel comfortable. Or as comfortable as she could when she was spending the evening with a man she would rather avoid.

Cal's appearance had taken her breath away, the dark grey suit tailored to him perfectly, the white shirt and light grey tie obviously both made of silk. His hair was brushed into some semblance of neatness tonight, but it was still too long, and even as Helen looked across the table from him now her fingers itched to reach out and smooth the waving darkness off his forehead.

Heaven knew what he would make of it if she didn't resist the impulse!

The memory of the kiss they had shared was in the dark blue of his eyes every time she looked at him, her heart beating a wild tattoo in her chest, her nerve-endings jangling warningly.

As if she needed any warning of the danger this man represented to her peace of mind!

'I'd like to order,' she bit out abruptly.

Cal gave a half-smile. 'Get it over with as quickly as you can, hm?'

Colour warmed her cheeks. 'I didn't want to be here in the first place, you know that,' she told him sharply, giving her own order to the waiter as he came to the table, keeping her face averted as Cal smoothly ordered his meal after her.

How on earth was she going to get through an entire evening with this man?

'Helen.'

There it was again, that gentle command in just the sound of her name, and she raised her eyes to his reluctantly.

'Let's just enjoy our meal, hmm?' he suggested softly. 'We can talk about Sam, if you like—he's a pretty neutral subject.'

As long as they kept off the subject of the little boy's grandparents; Helen didn't want to become any more involved in that situation than she already had been.

Talking about Sam turned out to be easier than she had thought, the little boy having crept into her affections on their brief acquaintance without her actually being aware of it. But she realised what had happened as she talked to Cal, could only silently regret that it *had* happened, knowing it would ultimately cause her pain.

It was a more relaxing evening than she had expected it to be, Cal deliberately setting out to put her at her ease, she was sure. And he succeeded, the two of them talking easily together as they left the restaurant a couple of hours later, Helen's defences down so much that she accepted when Cal offered her a drink at the main house.

It was only as they approached the house that Helen questioned the sense of her actions. She really shouldn't spend any time alone with Cal; it could be her undoing.

She knew it was even more of a mistake when Cal suggested she go with him to Sam's bedroom to check on the little boy. Sam lay on his back in the cot, spread-eagled on the mattress, his curls dark against the whiteness of the sheet beneath him, his lashes long and silky against his cheeks, his little pink rose-bud of a mouth falling open slackly as he breathed gently.

Helen's heart ached at the sight of him, and she turned away with a choked sob, attempting to cover the emotion with a low cough, excusing herself from the room as Cal looked at her concernedly.

'I don't want to wake him,' she whispered hurriedly before escaping from the nursery.

She leant weakly on the wall outside the room, drawing in deep, controlling breaths, flatly denying entry into her mind the memories seeing Sam like that had evoked.

'Are you all right?' Cal stood in front of her, his eyes dark with concern.

Helen took in a shuddering breath, looking up at him with shuttered eyes, although she still leant on the wall behind her for support, her legs feeling decidedly shaky. 'I—it was very hot in the nursery,' she excused firmly.

'Yes,' Cal agreed, although he didn't look convinced, watching her frowningly. 'Let's go down and have that drink,' he suggested lightly as she made no effort to add anything to her earlier statement.

She had intended having a coffee and then leaving, but the brandy Cal suggested once they got down to the sitting-room seemed much more appropriate, the first few sips going a long

way to settling her frayed nerves. Lord, she was
becoming a nervous wreck in just a few days!

'Better?' he prompted as he watched the
colour returning to her cheeks.

She swallowed hard. 'Much. Thanks.'

'I can't imagine my life without him now,'
Cal said softly.

Helen felt her cheeks drain of colour again.
'No,' she agreed hollowly.

Cal grimaced. 'They're so dependent on us
at that age.'

'Yes.'

'I don't suppose——'

'Cal, could we talk about something else?'
she cut in sharply, her movements agitated.

He hesitated for a moment, and then he relaxed slightly. 'I suppose I do sound a bit like
a doting father,' he dismissed self-derisively.
'I've enjoyed our dinner tonight, Helen,' he
told her softly, his gaze compelling her to look
up at him.

It was an impulse impossible to resist, and
she instantly found herself drowning in a sea
of dark blue.

'So have I.' It was impossible to lie to him
when he held her gaze so easily.

'On Saturday——'

'You do seem to hit on subjects I would
rather not go into,' she interrupted tautly.

'We can't just pretend it didn't happen.' He shrugged broad shoulders.

Helen looked at him challengingly. 'Why can't we?'

His mouth quirked. 'Can we?' he prompted sceptically.

'I can.' She lied without hesitation this time, knowing she had no choice; she didn't want to talk about what had happened between them on Saturday, didn't even want to think about it.

He shrugged. 'Then you're having better luck than I have; I can't seem to get it out of my mind.'

'Maybe you need to spend some time in London,' she scorned defensively. 'You're obviously missing the—companionship you can find there.'

'Does this usually work?'

Helen looked at him sharply. 'Does what usually work?' she echoed challengingly.

His mouth quirked; he was not in the least perturbed by the insult she had just given him. 'It must do.' He spoke almost to himself. 'Otherwise you wouldn't still be using it,' he mused.

'What are you talking about?' she said irritably.

'Attack being the best form of defence,' he drawled.

Her gaze wavered and fell guiltily away from his; she wasn't going to win with this man, she knew she wasn't.

'Helen,' he stood directly in front of her now, one hand moving under her chin to tilt her face up towards his, 'I am not in the habit of seeking—companionship, anywhere.' A gently teasing smile curved his lips. 'I am of an age where I'm looking for more than you are implying.' His smile became more intimate. 'Actually, I wasn't looking at all, had decided my own life could go on a back-burner for a while, or at least until Sam is completely settled with me. And now, here you are.' He shrugged at the mystery of life.

'I'll soon be gone again,' she reminded sharply, unsure of what he was saying, but knowing she had to dispel any doubts he might have to the contrary.

'Not for a couple of weeks.' He tapped her cheek in playful reproval. 'A lot can happen in two weeks.'

Not to her. Never to her.

'I don't think so,' she told him hardly.

'I don't think *either* of us should think at all for the moment,' Cal said briskly. 'I had heard so much about you from your father, had even seen photographs of you.' He shook his head. 'But I wasn't prepared for the flesh and blood you, hadn't expected this.'

'This?' she echoed impatiently.

'This.' He nodded, lowering his head to hers.

It was what she had been waiting for—and fearing—all evening, Helen knew that as her body curved snugly into the hardness of his.

Just as if it was where she was meant to be.

The hours that had elapsed since she had last been in his arms might never have been; her arms curved about his neck as their mouths fused together. His hands cupped either side of her face, tasting her lips slowly before claiming them with an agonised groan. His arms enfolded Helen against him, his hands caressing the length of her body, sending shivers of sensation wherever he touched.

Helen trembled with reaction, never having known this mindless desire, wanting to be closer to him, so close she didn't know where her body began and Cal's ended.

Her hands were entwined in the thick darkness of his hair, loving its silky softness, his body sensual to the touch, aware of her own effect on him as he quivered against her.

'Maybe I shouldn't have started this,' he groaned against her throat. 'But now that I have, I don't want it to stop!'

Neither did she, raising no objection as Cal gently removed the combs from her hair, framing her face with the loose blonde waves as he looked deeply into her eyes.

'Helen!' he said achingly as he saw his own desire reflected there, claiming her mouth tenderly now, in no hurry to rush the loving they knew they both wanted.

Helen returned his kisses, her whole body shaking with need, a need that was inevitable, had been from the moment they had first kissed.

This was what she had been trying to run away from since Saturday!

A warm lethargy entered her limbs, but at the same time her body was taut with wanting, her breath catching in her throat as Cal's hands caressed down the sides of her body, fingertips lightly brushing the tips of her breasts, her nipples hard with desire, red-hot pleasure coursing through her body as he repeated the caress again and again.

Helen had never known anything like this in her life before, knew that she was no longer in control, that desire had taken over, a desire that wouldn't be denied. It was the same for Cal, she knew that, could feel the hardness of his body against her as he made no effort to hide his need from her.

He raised his head, looking down at her with dark blue eyes. 'Helen?'

She knew what he was asking of her, knew he wouldn't take advantage of the desire between them if it wasn't what she wanted too.

She opened her mouth to speak. 'I——'

'Cal, I wondered if——' A brief knock had heralded the arrival of the man who now stood framed in the doorway, breaking off what he had been about to say as he realised he had interrupted them.

Helen couldn't see the man's face properly in the half-light of the hallway behind him, the lounge itself lit only by a small table-lamp some distance away from the door—and yet she had recognised the voice instantly.

The man standing in the doorway was Daniel Scott!

CHAPTER SEVEN

DANIEL'S presence here was enough to tell Helen she hadn't been mistaken on Friday at all, that it had been him she had seen driving down the lane near Cherry Trees after all.

And she didn't need to be a mathematician to work out that Daniel had to be the personal assistant/accountant that Cal had taken on to help him.

Daniel, of all people!

She had stepped back from Cal the moment the other man had knocked so briefly on the door, but she moved even further away from him now as Daniel eyed them speculatively.

Daniel had changed little since she had last been in his presence, still the handsome devil who had impressed her so easily six years ago, his hair thick and golden, brushed lightly back from his too-handsome face, the features almost too perfect; his eyes so light a blue they were almost grey, fringed by long dark lashes; his nose short and straight, with a sculptured mouth and strong determined jaw. He was wearing a loose grey sweater and fitted denims, the latter emphasising the muscled strength of his body.

He had a handsomeness that only seemed to increase with the years, thirty-five now. And yet Helen wasn't in the least impressed by him, not any more, knew him too well for that.

'I'm so sorry,' he apologised to Cal as he moved further into the room. 'I didn't realise you weren't alone.' The smile he gave Helen was speculative, to say the least.

Cal had recovered his composure quicker than Helen, and was in complete control again now, any irritation he might have felt at the interruption quickly masked, although his smile was a little strained.

'Helen, this is Daniel Scott, my new assistant,' he introduced smoothly. 'Daniel, this is Helen Foster, a friend of mine.'

Daniel thrust out his hand confidently. 'Miss Foster,' he acknowledged softly.

'Mr Scott.' She swallowed hard, touching his hand as briefly as good manners would allow.

A *friend*, hmm? Daniel's mocking gaze seemed to say as Helen continued to look at him with distaste.

Why did he have to judge everyone by his own standards? she fumed silently. Just because he had walked in and found her in Cal's arms it was no reason to jump to conclusions concerning their relationship. But that was typical of Daniel, as she well knew.

'What did you want to see me about?' Cal prompted with a politeness that was slightly belied by the irritation in his gaze.

'I had some papers here I wasn't too sure of.' Daniel indicated the sheets of paper in his hand. 'But they can wait until morning,' he dismissed with a shrug.

'Please, don't let me stop you,' Helen spoke directly to Cal, not wanting even to look at Daniel again, knowing what she would see in his eyes. And she had no intention of feeling self-conscious about something that was none of his business. 'I have to go now anyway.'

The moment between them had gone, they both knew that, and yet Cal looked as if he would like to ask her to stay, at least until Daniel had gone and they could say goodnight in private.

But Helen just wanted to get away, from both men, and regain her composure in peace. 'I really do have to go,' she said firmly before he could object. 'It's very late.'

And the question of time hadn't arisen until they had been so rudely interrupted, they both knew that. But Cal seemed to take one look at the determination on her face and decide not to argue with her.

'I'll walk to the door with you.' His tone brooked no argument to this suggestion.

Helen moved to the door, her movements disjointed, just wanting to escape now from what had become a very embarrassing situation.

'Goodnight, Miss Foster,' Daniel called softly from behind her.

She turned sharply at the mockery in his voice, her eyes flashing her dislike. 'Goodnight, Mr Scott,' she bit out tautly.

He nodded. 'I have no doubt we will meet again,' he said pleasantly enough, although Helen could clearly see the challenge in his eyes.

'No doubt,' she echoed sharply.

Cal closed the lounge door behind them, following closely behind Helen as she all but marched to the front door in her need to escape.

She turned as she reached the door. 'Thank you for dinner. It was——'

'Why so formal, Helen?' Cal looked puzzled. 'I realise it was a little embarrassing just now, but even so, I think we're past the stage where we have to be so distantly polite to each other.'

His gentle teasing did nothing to relax her; she just wanted to get away from here!

'I suppose so,' she acknowledged distractedly. 'But I really do have to go now.'

'Helen?' The soft query of her name made her look up at him with vague eyes. He looked at her searchingly for several seconds before giving a resigned sigh. 'I'll call you tomorrow, OK?' His gaze compelled her to answer in the affirmative.

A telephone call couldn't do any harm. Besides, she had a feeling that if she didn't let him call her he would come round to the house, and she could refuse him all the more easily over the telephone. Because she had no intention of going out with him again. It had been bad enough before she knew of Daniel's presence in Cal's house, but now it was impossible!

'All right,' she nodded abruptly. 'Tomorrow,' she accepted.

His hand under her chin gently raised her face to his. 'Drive carefully,' he murmured against her mouth before his lips softly touched hers.

She didn't feel like driving at all once she had got behind the wheel of her car, reaction beginning to set in in earnest now.

Daniel of all people, *here*.

He was the last person she would ever have imagined moving to the country. And now that he had she wished it could have been anywhere but near her home.

The less she saw of him, the better!

* * *

'That was Cal again.' Her father looked at her reprovingly. 'I can't keep telling him you're out,' he added irritably.

It was the third time Cal had telephoned today, she knew, and yet she just didn't want to talk to him.

Shocked reaction had set in after seeing Daniel again after all this time, and she needed to be left in peace to sort out her confused thoughts. Most of all she needed to stay away from anything that reminded her Daniel was in the neighbourhood at all, and Cal could do that all too easily. After all, if it weren't for him Daniel wouldn't be in the area.

Worst of all, she felt conscience-bound to warn Cal about Daniel, and yet how to do it, that was her worry now. She certainly couldn't pretend she didn't know anything about his background; it might not be exactly black, but it was certainly shaded in grey! And she had a feeling Cal wouldn't want a man like that working for him.

Or would he? The man she had thought him to be two weeks ago wouldn't have been in the least concerned by an employee's shady past, as long as it was now working in his favour; had she really changed her mind about him so much that she no longer believed that to be true? As far as Daniel and his working for Cal went, she knew the answer to that was yes, but she still thought he had been underhand about his dealings with her father over Cherry Trees.

But none of that solved her problem here and now of Cal's third telephone call today.

She came to a decision. 'Well, if he calls again you won't be telling a lie,' she said firmly. 'Because I am going out!'

'Helen——'

'Not now, Daddy,' she warned tautly, her emotions fraught with tension.

'But, darling——'

'I'll talk to you later.' Her voice gentled slightly. 'I promise.'

She couldn't tell even him all of what had taken place last night; although after Cal's telephone calls today he must already have a pretty good idea!

She would have to tell her father of Daniel's presence at Cal's house; knowing, as her father did, of her involvement with the other man in the past, it would be awful if her father should meet him by chance and realise exactly who he was. Especially if she hadn't yet told Cal!

'All right,' her father sighed. 'But I must say you're acting very oddly.'

She knew he meant out of character, her usual cool calm completely absent today. But she had been so completely shaken by what had happened last night, and of the abrupt ending to the evening.

She still couldn't quite believe the cruelty of fate that had thrown Daniel into her life once again. Her avoidance of him these last few years, while it hadn't been exactly deliberate, hadn't been unplanned either. It had been all too easy not to frequent the places she knew he would choose to spend his evenings, and on a professional level she hadn't cared whether their paths had crossed or not, knowing, as she did, that her personal integrity far outweighed any success he might appear to have made. By some lucky quirk Helen had managed not to see him for the last six years. Now, with his proximity, it was going to take all of her ingenuity *not* to see him!

Her favourite cove was out of the question for her worried wanderings today, as she remembered all too well how Cal had so easily found her there last time. Remembering that, he might try to locate her there again today.

But she needed to be near the sea, its deliberate inevitability a balm to her frayed nerves.

Nothing about her own life these last few weeks had seemed inevitable; she had been sure that without too much effort on her part she need never see Daniel Scott again, had been even more sure that a man like Caleb Jones had appeared to be could never affect her deepest emotions in any way.

She had been wrong on both counts.

Oh, this unexpected meeting with Daniel again after all this time was disquieting enough, but to acknowledge, even to herself, the growing attraction she felt towards Cal was totally devastating. She had at least thought she liked Daniel before believing herself in love with him; she still wasn't sure she actually liked Cal, only that he affected her more than any other man she had ever known.

The cove she finally found was even more private than her usual refuge, and as she clambered down among the rocks she felt a sense of peace washing over her, the complications of her life unimportant for the couple of hours she spent there just enjoying the gentle uprush and ebb of the grey-blue water.

Nothing had really changed about her purpose here, she realised; she still had to persuade her father that Cherry Trees was their family home, and should remain that way. Oh, Daniel's presence here was a complication she hadn't expected, but she had no reason to suppose he was any more eager to see her again than she was him. As for this attraction that seemed to have sprung up between Cal and herself... She was a grown woman, wasn't she, quite capable of dealing with that complication? She and Cal were completely unsuited as a couple, and a purely physical relationship had never appealed to her. Those decisions made, she returned home with a determined resolve.

She was quite unprepared for Cal's presence in the garden with her father, Sam playing happily at their feet as they enjoyed an early evening drink together!

Dark blue eyes studied her guardedly as she strode purposefully across the lawn towards them, only a slight, but brief, hesitancy in her step showing she was in the least disconcerted by his presence here, before she continued her progress across the garden bathed in early evening sunshine.

Sam looked up from his digging of the flowerbed as he sensed her presence, his face instantly lighting up with pleasure. 'Lennie!' he cried gleefully, raising his arms towards her to be picked up.

Only the hardest of hearts could remain unmoved by such spontaneity, and, although Helen knew she shielded her emotions from hurt, she couldn't remain immune to the happiness in those baby-blue eyes, bending down to pick the little boy up, giving a tearful smile as he planted a shy kiss on her cheek.

'Nothing but seeing you again would do.' Cal had stood up to move to her side, talking softly as Sam buried his face shyly against her neck. 'He's talked of nothing else but you since Saturday.'

She felt sure that had pleased the little boy's grandparents, at least his grandmother! They couldn't possibly realise from that what little real significance she had in Sam's life.

'Only because I took him to see the animals at the zoo.' She tickled the little boy in her arms until he squirmed amid giggles of laughter. 'Sam's as mercenary as the next child, aren't you, baby?' she teased him. 'He's hoping I'll take him there again.'

'Maybe,' Cal acknowledged a little sheepishly. 'Although he has genuinely taken a liking to you,' he added seriously.

'And I like you too, little man.' She held the baby close against her, fighting off the pain of familiarity as memories washed over her. The smile she bestowed on the child was a little more strained now. 'Has anyone thought to offer you a drink, I wonder?' she drily rebuked the two men, with their long, cooling glasses of whisky and water.

'He's already drunk all of his lemonade.' Her father held up the empty feeding cup with knowing satisfaction. 'But if you're hinting you would like a drink I'll go into the house and get you some fresh orange.' He stood up.

The last thing Helen wanted was to be left alone with Cal, but a refusal of the offered drink would show that all too obviously. And she was supposed to be a mature woman of

twenty-six, and surely past the stage of re-
sisting being alone with any man!

'Lovely,' she accepted with a tight smile in
her father's direction, all the more annoyed because he knew exactly what he was doing.

Cal took a step closer to her as her father
entered the house. 'You wouldn't take my calls.'
It was a statement rather than an accusation.

She didn't look up at him. 'I've been out,'
she returned softly, all the time smiling at Sam.

'Not all day,' he rebuked gently.

Helen's eyes flashed deeply green as she
glared up at him. 'Part of it,' she defended.

'After my calls became impossible to ignore,'
he said drily.

'I don't have to explain myself to you,' she
flared.

He looked at her consideringly for several
seconds, before nodding slowly. 'No, you
don't,' he acknowledged softly. 'But you did
say I could call you,' he reminded her.

Her cheeks became flushed. She had accepted the possibility of his telephoning her
before she had spent a night telling herself how
impossible the situation was. Daniel's presence
here was merely a complication to a situation
she already knew was fast hurtling out of
control. Daniel was just a very timely reminder
of how becoming emotionally involved with
people became a very painful experience. And

falling for a man like Cal could be even more devastating than believing herself in love with Daniel had proved to be all those years ago; Cal had the added complication of Sam for her to deal with.

She shrugged dismissively. 'So I changed my mind,' she challenged.

Cal looked as if he would like to lean forward and shake her, but he instantly resisted the temptation, his gaze resting on Sam as he sat so confidently in her arms.

'So you did,' Cal said heavily. 'Running away from our emotions is never the answer, you know, Helen,' he added softly.

Her mouth set angrily, two vivid spots of colour in her cheeks now. 'You don't know what you're talking about,' she snapped. He couldn't know about Daniel, he just couldn't! Unless her father——? But no, he didn't know yet that Daniel was working for the other man. At least, she hadn't told him... 'Has my father said something to you?' she demanded sharply, her eyes narrowed.

Cal shrugged. 'Some things don't need to be said. I'm sorry that you had to go through something like that, but you can't let it colour your whole life.'

He didn't know about Daniel specifically, but he knew enough to realise someone had hurt her very badly in the past!

'How I deal with the pain in my life is my business,' she bit out tautly.

'Not if it affects what's between us.' He shook his head.

Helen looked at him scathingly, her guard well back in place now. 'There's nothing between us,' she snapped. 'Physical attraction——'

'There's more to it than that and you know it,' Cal cut in determinedly.

'I don't know any—— Oh, look, Sam, here comes Uncle David with my orange juice.' She quickly changed her angry denial as her father came out of the house, dampening down the emotion with effort. 'Thanks.' She accepted the glass of juice, deftly avoiding meeting her father's searching gaze. He had already played too big a part in involving her in this situation, and it had to stop. Now. 'I have to go in and wash my hair,' she excused herself firmly, handing Sam back to Cal, deftly avoiding too much contact with him as she did so, although she could see by the knowing look in those dark blue eyes that he was completely aware of what she had done. But that didn't matter; the sooner he accepted the situation, the better, as far as she was concerned.

'Couldn't that wait until later?' her father prompted hardly, a reproving look on his face.

Helen ignored that look; Cal was his guest, not hers! 'You know how long it takes for me to dry my hair,' she insisted lightly.

'Sam.' The little boy held out his arms towards her.

'I think he wants to come and watch,' Cal explained drily.

'I don't—I——' She became flustered in the warmth of Cal's gaze as he told her without words that he clearly remembered last night when her hair had been loose about her shoulders, his hands buried in its thickness as he kissed her. It was scraped back today in the severe plait down her spine that her father so hated, and she could see Cal felt the same way about it as his gaze lingered on the blonde tresses.

'Sam,' the little boy said again, more firmly this time.

'By coincidence I was reading him the story of Rapunzel last night when I put him to bed,' Cal murmured softly. 'He doesn't really take in the stories, but he's obviously remembered enough of this one to be interested in the letting down of your hair.'

'It isn't long enough for anyone to climb up,' she returned tautly, taking Sam into her arms.

Only long enough for him to bury his face in its scented thickness, Cal's warm gaze seemed to say.

She turned away abruptly, knowing she was once again becoming seduced by those deep blue eyes. It just wasn't fair after all the arguments she had given herself today for not becoming involved with him!

'Excuse us.' She spoke to neither man in particular, talking softly to Sam as they went into the house.

The telephone was ringing as she walked through the hallway, and she picked up the receiver with an apologetic smile at Sam as she put him down on the floor. At least she knew it couldn't be Cal calling once again to disturb her calm existence.

She recited the telephone number automatically, keeping a close eye on Sam as he wandered off into the lounge.

'Hello, Helen,' greeted an all too familiar voice. 'I think we should meet, don't you?'

Daniel, she realised instantly.

Here was someone else who had the power to shake up her ordered world!

CHAPTER EIGHT

HELEN's hand tightly gripped the receiver, her fingernails digging into her palm where she held it so firmly.

How dared he call her here? was her instant reaction. Discounting the fact that he had acquired her telephone number at all, he had no right to call her at her father's home. No matter what he felt the urgency to be.

Although he didn't sound as if he had been at all disturbed by her presence here. But remembering his cool self-confidence of the past she thought that was probably true.

All the more reason to give the impression it was of no importance to her either. 'I can't imagine why you should think that,' she returned coolly, 'when I've had nothing to say to you for almost six years.'

'I'm flattered you should remember how long ago it is since we last met,' he murmured softly.

He wasn't flattered at all, knew she had good reason never to forget his part in her life! 'I thought you would have gone much further up the professional ladder during that time than you actually have,' she said challengingly.

'I wouldn't have thought PA to a man like Caleb Jones was backsliding,' Daniel bit back tautly, obviously stung by the taunt.

'It's a good job,' she granted dismissively. 'But I would have thought you would have your own accountancy firm by now.'

'Maybe I don't care for the responsibility,' he rasped.

And maybe things weren't going quite so well for him now as they had been all those years ago. She hadn't particularly been aware of any talk of him among her colleagues, but it soon became known in that tight circle which of them it might be best to avoid employing. It would also go a long way to explaining his presence here in the countryside, when he had always professed to hate it so much.

'I have nothing to say to you, Daniel.' She sighed at the waste he had made of his undoubted talents.

'I believe it might be in the best interests of both of us if we did meet,' he said insistently.

Helen frowned; what could he possibly mean by that remark?

'Let's meet and discuss it,' he told her when she voiced her concern.

'Discuss what?' she prompted irritably.

'Not over the telephone, Helen,' he returned briskly. 'Perhaps I could meet you for dinner tomorrow evening? Or will you be seeing Cal then?' he added mockingly.

'None of your damned business!' she snapped. 'I——' She broke off as a crash sounded in the lounge. Oh, lord, *Sam*! She had forgotten all about the wandering baby in her agitation, and she had had the nerve to rebuke Cal for his negligence of the little boy the first time they had met; she was no better when the provocation was deep enough. 'I have to go,' she told Daniel abruptly.

'Dinner, tomorrow, eight o'clock, at the Bowling Green Inn,' he managed to say quickly before she put the receiver down to go to Sam.

The baby was standing in front of the fireplace with a guilty look on his face as he looked up at her, tears balanced on the edge of his long lashes ready to fall, an ornamental china robin in two pieces on the fireplace at his feet.

It didn't take much imagination to realise that Sam had reached up on to the high mantel for the robin, lost his balance and somehow dropped the treasured bird.

'It's all right, Sam,' Helen instantly reassured him as his bottom lip trembled precariously, going down on her haunches so that she was on the same level as him. 'A bit of glue and the robin will be as good as new.' She smiled at him.

'Sam notty.' He still looked forlorn, his head hung in shame.

Helen had to bite her lip to stop herself laughing at Sam's accurate description of himself as 'naughty'; it was obviously an expression he had heard about himself many times before! And no doubt his action was a little naughty, for the little boy was obviously aware that he shouldn't have touched the ornament at all, but who could possibly be cross with him when he looked so adorable in his contrition? Certainly not her.

'A little bit,' she admitted consideringly. 'But you won't do it again, will you?'

He shook his head gravely, the incident forgotten as far as he was concerned as she suggested they go upstairs and wash her hair now.

It was obvious from his curiosity that he had never been upstairs in the house before, going from room to room in open nosiness once they were upstairs.

As soon as they reached Helen's bathroom it became clear he had lost all interest in watching her wash her hair, pulling at his clothes with the intention of taking a bath.

Helen laughed softly in defeat of his determination as she ran the bath water for him; there was obviously a lot of his uncle in the little boy!

She sobered slightly as she thought of Cal's own stubbornness. Now, more than ever, with Daniel being awkward, she didn't want to become involved with the other man, felt threatened by one and deeply disturbed by the other, and neither emotion was a comfortable one.

'I'm so glad you decided to come after all,' Daniel said smoothly from across the table in the restaurant booth.

It hadn't been a question of *'deciding'* any-thing; she hadn't had any choice but to come here this evening. If she hadn't turned up at all she knew Daniel well enough to realise he would make trouble over it. And she hadn't been able to telephone the house to tell him she wouldn't be coming because Cal might have taken the call. And Daniel had been well aware of that.

'What do you want, Daniel?' she said wearily, not prepared to play games with him.

'Shall we order?' he returned lightly.

'I didn't come here to eat——'

'It is a restaurant,' he mocked, grey-blue eyes dancing with mischief.

He was still so handsome, even more so in the dark suit and pale grey shirt he wore to-night. But Helen was unmoved as she looked at him, knew that this outward charm was a deceit, not fooled for a moment by the warmth of his smile.

'I'm not hungry,' she snapped impatiently. 'Now what do you want to talk to me about?'

He turned the charm of his smile on the waitress as she appeared at the side of their table. 'Yes, we're ready to order now,' he said smoothly. 'Prawns Marie-Rose and a crispy duck with salad to follow for the lady,' he ordered over Helen's gasp at his audacity. She didn't hear what he ordered for himself in her amazement that he had remembered her own preferences after all this time. 'You do still like prawns and duck, I hope?' he murmured huskily once the waitress had gone.

'Yes...' She shook her head irritably. 'That isn't the point——'

'I can order you something else if you would prefer it,' he put in calmly, looking at her enquiringly.

'I would *prefer* it if we weren't having this conversation at all!' She glared at him.

He sobered, his expression suddenly one of anger rather than the amused indulgence with her discomfort he had been displaying since she had arrived at the restaurant ten minutes earlier. Daniel had already been seated at the table when she had arrived, and she had sat down only long enough to tell him she wouldn't be staying, wasn't even dressed for an evening out, her trousers and deep green blouse smart but certainly not suitable for dining out in. He had somehow managed to manoeuvre it so that their meal was ordered, and a bottle of wine was already being opened beside their table.

'I would prefer it too,' he rasped once the wine waiter had gone. 'But I'm sure you'll agree we have to talk.'

'I can't think what about,' Helen snapped. 'I said all I had to say to you almost six years ago!'

'And it's concerning that very thing that we have to talk now.' He nodded curtly, his nostrils flared in anger.

Helen frowned. Maybe she was a little dense tonight; she had slept badly the night before, had been sleeping badly since her arrival actually, and she had felt uncomfortable lying to her father earlier when she had told him she was going out for a drive; she certainly had no idea what Daniel and she could possibly have left to talk about!

'I think the past is best left forgotten,' she told him abruptly, not wanting to dwell on her past humiliation; it had taken her most of the last five and a half years to try and get over that.

'My feelings exactly.' Daniel nodded determinedly, his expression grim.

She frowned her puzzlement. 'Then——'

'Completely forgotten,' he added pointedly.

'You're the one who keeps bringing it up,' she pointed out impatiently.

'I mean all of it, Helen,' he bit out coldly, all the smooth charm gone now. 'Not just our past relationship.'

Her brow cleared as she at last realised what he meant. She had as much as decided, out of loyalty for her father's friendship with Cal, that she would have to say something to Cal about what she knew concerning Daniel's past dealings. How to approach the subject, without mentioning her own involvement with Daniel, had been her main problem. She could see from Daniel's expression that he was very worried about her doing just that.

She shook her head. 'I don't think I can do that,' she shrugged ruefully.

'Why the hell not?' he rasped, his eyes narrowed with fury.

'Cal has a right to know——'

'I did nothing illegal,' Daniel cut in forcefully.

'It was immoral!' she insisted firmly.

'That doesn't necessarily mean it was a crime,' he scorned.

She was well aware of the fact that nothing he had done had been a criminal offence; if it had been she would have done something about it.

'Cal——'

'Just how close *are* you and Cal?' he interrupted speculatively.

'None of your damned business!' Her cheeks were flushed with anger.

'You looked close enough to me the other night,' Daniel taunted.

'I told you,' she said in an evenly controlled voice. 'My relationship with Cal is none of your business.'

'Oh, but I think it is.' Some of his anger had faded now, and he was back in control again.

Her mouth tightened. 'If you think our past relationship——'

'Oh, that has only a little to do with it,' he mocked. 'It's the relationship we have now that is important.'

'We don't have a relationship now,' she denied vehemently.

'Exactly,' Daniel taunted.

Helen gave an impatient sigh. 'What *are* you talking about?' She gave the waitress an irritated frown as she placed their starters on the table in front of them, the other woman scuttling away timidly in the face of such vehement displeasure. Helen gave Daniel a scathing look. 'Could we just get this over with so that I can leave? I certainly have no intention of eating this meal!'

'Please yourself.' He shrugged uncon-
cernedly, relaxing back on his side of the booth.
'You see, Helen, after the other night we don't
even know each other.'

'Daniel——'

'The moment you returned my formal
greeting as if we had only just met for the first
time you made it virtually impossible to ever
admit to knowing me six years ago.' His head
went back in triumph, challenging her to
dispute his claim. 'If you try to tell Cal any
differently now he's going to wonder why you
didn't come straight out with the truth the other
evening, will probably think that you were involved in those past deals too.'

Helen paled, realising just how easily she had
played into this man's hands.

She stood up abruptly.

Daniel's eyes narrowed as she picked up her
bag. 'What are you doing?'

She didn't even bother to answer him,
walking out of the restaurant, ignoring the
waitress's worried look in her direction as she
went out of the door; let Daniel explain—if he
could!—her reasons for leaving.

She felt sick, knowing that the situation was
of her own making. But she had been so surprised to see Daniel at Cal's the other evening
that her responses to him had been mechanical
rather than devised.

But it was just like Daniel to want to take advantage of her disconcertion. He had always been one to recognise the best and easiest way out for himself.

Her father gave her a piercing look as she let herself back into the house, putting down his newspaper as she seemed preoccupied and ill at ease. 'Have you been to see Cal?' he queried softly.

She looked at him sharply. 'Cal?' she echoed in a puzzled voice; she had avoided being alone with the other man last night, until he had finally had to give in and leave with Sam, the little boy tired out. The telephone had been noticeably silent all day, so it seemed Cal had taken the hint that she didn't even want to talk to him. 'Why on earth should you think I've been to see Cal?' She frowned at her father.

He gave a wry smile. 'Because you always have that harassed look when you've been talking to him.'

She sighed at the truth of that; her father couldn't possibly know there was now someone else in the area who could upset her even more than Cal did, in a completely different way.

'No,' she said heavily. 'I haven't seen Cal tonight.'

He looked at her consideringly. 'Then what has upset you?'

Her father was too astute, knew her far too well, to be fobbed off with a half-hearted explanation. Besides, he would have to know about Daniel's being here sooner or later... The only consolation to telling her father was that he didn't know the full story of her breakup with Daniel; he hadn't been in any sort of emotional state himself at the time to be burdened with her humiliating misjudgement as well as her heartache over loving a man who had let her down. Her father had believed then, and still believed, that Daniel had callously ended their relationship because he was no longer interested in her, and had no idea she had been the one to tell Daniel she no longer wanted any part of his life.

The expression on her father's face darkened when she told him about the other man now working for Cal.

'It was just a surprise to see him again,' she dismissed abruptly. 'The other stupidity is just an embarrassment.' She had told her father of her initial reaction of acting as if she had never met Daniel before. 'I would just feel such a fool admitting the truth to Cal now.' She shrugged with more calm than she felt; Daniel could make her look more than a fool if he was crossed. Lord, how she had ever thought herself in love with such a man was beyond her. Her only possible excuse was that, like her father, she had been vulnerable at that time in her life. And that wasn't really any excuse for being taken in by a man like Daniel had turned out to be.

'Well, if Daniel is happy not to admit to the relationship too, it shouldn't prove a problem.' Her father shrugged, although he didn't look very happy about the situation himself.

Daniel was more than happy not to admit to the relationship!

'I feel uncomfortable about it.' She made a face.

'So do I,' he admitted needlessly. 'But I don't suppose it's necessary for Cal to know...'

Now she had put her father in an awkward position too! 'If you would rather I told him——'

'No,' he cut in abruptly, standing up. 'But I just hope Scott stays out of my way,' he said grimly. 'I remember what you were like six years ago after he had let you down, and——' He broke off as the doorbell rang. 'I wonder who that is,' he muttered vaguely as he went to answer the door.

Cal. She knew it instinctively.

She met his gaze unflinchingly as he came into the room ahead of her father, although she felt as if her duplicity were stamped all over her face.

He looked breathtakingly handsome in a light blue shirt worn beneath a checked jacket, his denims faded from wear rather then affectation, his dark hair once again ruffled from the light breeze outside.

'I wondered if you would care to come out for a drink.' He came straight to the point, probably sensing that her mood was not a patient one.

On top of her empty stomach—she hadn't been able to eat before she went out to meet Daniel either!—it would probably make her ill. And yet she somehow felt the need to be with him, felt as if she had a heavy weight hanging over her head just waiting to fall on her. And once it did she knew there would be no more invitations like this one. Far from her wanting to stay away from Cal, Daniel's threat to her now made her realise how much she really wanted to do the opposite. This incomprehensible desire for Cal was even more ridiculous than the way she had once felt about Daniel, and yet to have her relationship with Cal threatened by the other man took all the fight against the relationship out of her.

'I'd like that,' she accepted huskily.

She didn't know who was more surprised by her easy acquiescence, her father or Cal!

'If you could see your faces,' she mocked.

'Take her out before she changes her mind,' her father advised Cal.

'I intend to.' Cal grasped hold of her arm and led her out of the house, hardly able to believe his luck.

'There's no rush,' she laughed as he bundled her into the Range Rover he had driven over in.

His gaze was dark. 'How do you know?'

She blushed at the desire in his eyes, his meaning obvious. For once she offered no argument, warmed by her own need to be in his arms.

It was ridiculous, totally illogical after the way she had been fighting against him, and yet she knew that of the two men Daniel was by far the most destructive and selfish. She wasn't sure how she felt about Cal any more.

But being in his arms proved more difficult tonight than at any other time! Cal actually did want to take her out for a drink, choosing a quiet little inn about ten miles drive away. The evening was still clear and warm, and they decided to take their second round of drinks out into the garden.

Cal gave a sigh of satisfaction as they seated themselves opposite each other around a table shaded by a multi-coloured umbrella. 'I can't remember the last time I felt relaxed enough to do this.' He took a thirst-quenching sip of his beer.

'Drink warm beer and swat gnats away before they bite you?' she teased, sipping her own fruit juice with only slightly less relish; it was turning out to be one of the hottest summers they had had for a long time.

He gave her a reproving look. 'The beer is deliciously cold,' he drawled contradictorily. 'And I'm rarely troubled with gnat bites.'

'But I am!' She swatted ineffectually at one of the insects, knowing that, no matter how hard she tried to keep them off her, later to-night she would find her skin speckled with their bites. 'I just seem to attract them,' she said disgustedly.

Cal looked concerned. 'We can sit inside, if you would prefer it?'

'No, of course not.' She smiled. 'Why should I deprive the gnats of the feast they are obviously promising themselves right now?' she added ruefully.

He laughed softly. 'Any comment I make to follow that remark would only be misconstrued!'

Warmth coloured her cheeks. He might not have taken her into his arms yet, but he obviously wanted to. It gave her a sense of antici-pation as they continued to laze in the late evening sunshine.

'I'm hoping to have quite a lot of the pressure taken off me in the next few weeks,' Cal said with pleasure. 'The man I've taken on to help me out seems to be quite capable. But of course, you've met him, haven't you?' He raised dark brows.

All thoughts of relaxing instantly deserted Helen, and she sat up stiffly. 'Have I?' she said sharply.

Cal's mouth quirked. 'I remember his interruption of the other evening only too well,' he reminded self-derisively.

'Oh, that,' she realised with some relief, although she didn't relax. Was that really what Cal meant, or was he testing her in some way? He couldn't know about Daniel, could he?

His mouth twisted ruefully. 'I wish I could dismiss it so easily; at the time I felt slightly murderous towards him!'

'It didn't show,' she said almost coyly. Coyly? Her? She didn't remember ever being *coy*! But then she had never met anyone quite like Cal before, she acknowledged reluctantly.

Cal shrugged. 'The man had only been working for me a day; I thought I should allow him a little more time to appreciate what is important to me before bawling him out for it.' He gave a rueful grimace.

Important to him? Was she?

'How is he working out?' She forced a casualness into her voice that wasn't really there; it would solve a lot of problems if Daniel was to prove unsuitable for Cal.

'He seems OK so far,' Cal dismissed. 'Only time will really tell if Daniel can adapt to our unusual working conditions. He's been used to working in the city, to normal office hours; he's going to find it very different working for me.'

She should have known that Daniel's work would be up to standard. There could be no doubt about his professional skills; it was his professional *ethics* that she had questioned. All that she could hope for was that his natural aversion to being in the countryside would eventually take precedence. Otherwise she was going to feel very uncomfortable every time she came home to see her father.

'I wish you had been willing to consider the job.' Cal looked at her ruefully.

'I still don't think that would have been a good idea.' But for different reasons now! The way their relationship was developing, it wouldn't have been wise for them to work together too.

'Possibly not,' he considered, his eyes warm. 'Are you ready to leave?'

She had been ready for the last hour! Although it had been pleasant enough, dangerously so; she hadn't wanted to argue with him once!

The silence between them in the Range Rover was companionable on the drive back rather than awkward, although Helen could feel her anticipation rising as they neared home.

'Care for a nightcap?' Cal asked huskily.

Remembering what had happened last time she went to his home, Helen knew she didn't want a repeat of that. She wanted to avoid seeing Daniel again at all if she could.

'Let's go to Cherry Trees,' she suggested lightly. 'Daddy can join us too then.'

Cal gave her a searching look in the last of the day's light, as if looking for a reluctance on her part to spend time alone with him. He seemed satisfied with what he read in her face, nodding agreement.

The lights were still on in the house when they got there, although Helen knew as soon as she went inside that her father had already gone to bed, the television silent, the lights only left on for her return.

'Coffee? Or something stronger?' She looked at Cal enquiringly.

'Actually, I'm not worried about either.' He smiled. 'Unless you would like something?'

She wasn't particularly worried about a drink either, but it was a little ridiculous neither of them wanting one when that was supposed to be the reason they were here at all!

She shook her head, suddenly feeling very self-conscious. 'I won't bother,' she said abruptly.

'But if you would like——'

'Really, Cal,' she laughed. 'Stop being so polite, I'm not used to it!'

He grinned. 'As I remember it, you were usually the one who was impolite.'

Her smile faded. 'I had good reason——'

'You think you had.' He moved across the room to tap her lightly on the nose. 'Things aren't always what they appear.'

No, she had realised that concerning her ideas about Sam's possibly being Cal's son. She knew now that wasn't true, but from initial appearances it had seemed a possibility to her. Could she be just as wrong about his plans concerning Cherry Trees? But she didn't see how she could be when her father seemed intent on selling and Cal seemed just as keen to buy the house.

Cal had watched the emotions flickering across her face, giving a rueful sigh. 'Could we not talk about that just now?'

'We have to talk about it some time,' she reminded herself as much as him; it was the reason she was here, after all.

'But not now,' Cal insisted firmly, caressing the side of her face with his thumbtip.

No, not now, she accepted achingly, moving willingly into his arms, her face raised to his as she returned his kiss. If anything she was more deeply affected than the last time she had been in his arms; the movement of his lips against hers was sweet torture.

Cal raised his head with a husky laugh. 'David is probably imagining all sorts of things going on down here now that it's gone quiet.'

Helen couldn't help smiling herself; it was like being two teenagers stealing illicit time together. 'It's more likely he's gone to sleep with a smug smile on his face,' she said drily.

'Or that he's resting himself ready for tomorrow,' Cal murmured indulgently, his arm resting along the back of the sofa behind her as they sat down.

She looked up at him enquiringly. 'Tomorrow?'

'Believe it or not, I used to weigh a stone more than I do now,' he grimaced.

'Yes?' Helen frowned her puzzlement with the statement.

'Your father will probably have lost weight too after running around after Sam for a couple of days,' he said with a shrug.

Helen stiffened. What did he mean by that remark?

Cal turned to her enquiringly at her prolonged silence, frowning a little at the incomprehension on her face. 'He didn't tell you?' he said slowly.

She was so tense now she felt as if she might break, the pleasant interlude in his arms over in the face of this new threat to her peace of mind. 'Tell me what?' she pushed tautly. But she knew. She *knew*.

Cal sat forward on the sofa as she stood up restlessly, his elbows resting on his knees as he looked up at her with concern. 'I have to go to London for a few days, a legal matter, and David has offered to have Sam here while I'm away,' he explained almost reluctantly.

Exactly what she had thought he meant! Sam here, in this house, playing, sleeping, just being here. She didn't know if she would be able to bear it.

Cal stood up and came across the room to her, grasping her shoulders. 'David said it would be all right,' he muttered almost to himself. 'But it isn't, is it?' he said heavily. 'Damn it, I had no idea it would affect you like this, or I would never have asked . . . I should have realised it might be too much for you.' He shook his head in self-disgust at his thoughtlessness.

Helen looked at him sharply. 'What do you mean?'

Her heart was beating a wild tattoo in her chest; her hands felt clammy and yet cold at the same time.

Cal gave a deep sigh, as if regretting what he was about to say, and yet knowing he had to say it none the less. 'I know about Ben, Helen,' he told her gently. 'David told me about him months ago.'

Ben. Oh, lord, how just the mention of his name could still hurt her!

Ben. As beautiful as Sam, but fated to die despite all her efforts for it to be otherwise. A precious child who hadn't lived to see his first birthday.

CHAPTER NINE

HELEN moved abruptly away from Cal, putting some distance between them as she went to stand in front of the window, staring out with sightless eyes, her hands twisting together in her agitation.

She put her head back, stiffening her shoulders, although she couldn't turn and look at Cal, her eyes filled with unshed tears, even now, after all these years.

'What did my father tell you?' she asked flatly.

Cal seemed to sense that she wouldn't let him near her, standing where she had left him. 'I had to know, Helen, otherwise I might have said or done something unthinkingly that would have hurt David in a way I wouldn't have been able to understand.'

She closed her eyes, swallowing hard. 'Yes,' she finally managed to choke out.

'Helen——'

'Please *don't*!' she almost shouted, her hands held up defensively as he would have come to her. She couldn't bear for him to touch her, would have broken down if he did. 'That year—it was the worst time I've ever known in my life,' she said shakily.

Much worse than anything Daniel could ever have done to her, touching her in a way that Daniel never could, although she acknowledged that it was because she had already been hurting so much that Daniel had been able to reach her in the way that he had. Maybe if she hadn't already been in such pain she would have been able to see through him from the first.

Cal drew in a ragged breath. 'In a way I can understand, although I was lucky, I still have Sam,' he said thankfully.

Of course. He had lost his brother and his brother's wife. Suddenly. With no warning at all. They hadn't really known what would happen, but she and her father had had more warning of what was to come than Cal could have done.

'I'm sorry,' she trembled. 'I didn't think.'

'As I said,' he shrugged, 'I was luckier than you and David, I still have Sam.'

And they had had Ben for almost a year. A year when they had almost lost him several times. But he had fought back, until that fateful day only eleven months after his birth when he hadn't been able to fight any more. It had broken Helen's heart to sit and watch him die.

'You were very close to your mother?'

She closed her eyes as fresh pain washed over her, taking her breath away.

Her mother. Tall and beautiful, her hair still naturally blonde, green eyes full of laughter, of a love of life. But she had lost that life giving birth to the son she and Helen's father had longed for for so long.

The pregnancy had been so unexpected, a complete surprise in her mother's fortieth year, none of them believing there would be another child after all these years; after all, Helen had been over eighteen by this time. The excitement for all of them when what Elizabeth Foster had believed to be an early 'change of life' had turned out to be a pregnancy!

It had been such an easy pregnancy too, closely monitored because of her mother's age, but there had been nothing to warn them of her mother's heart defect that only showed itself at the height of labour, causing her heart to stop and never begin beating again; no warning either that Ben would have that same heart defect, except to a greater degree. The double tragedy had been all the harder to bear because the problem had never shown itself before, Helen born a normal, healthy child after a relatively easy labour.

But it wasn't to be a second time—her mother's heart had been strained too much, although she had never known that her son would only live another eleven months before he too died.

Helen's father had been devastated by his wife's death, theirs a marriage of love and laughter, and Helen's grief had only been slightly less because her time was so occupied with taking care of a very sick baby.

With her father unable to deal with the baby at all for the first few weeks of Ben's life, his desolation at losing her mother almost crippling him, Helen's closeness to Ben had been complete. She had fought so hard to keep him alive. But it had been a fight that the doctors and specialists had warned her she was destined to lose. Although it hadn't stopped her trying to win.

Her heartbreak at Ben's death had been so deep that she'd had to get away, completely away from anything that reminded her of him and the happy family she had once known, which was why she had originally gone to London. Where she had ultimately met Daniel and been hurt all over again.

'Yes,' she said heavily. 'I was very close to my mother.'

Cal shook his head. 'David told me how you bore the responsibility of Ben when he was too broken to cope with anything.'

She swallowed hard. 'Could we talk about something else?'

She hadn't realised Cal had moved until she felt his hands on her shoulders turning her towards him. But at his first touch her control broke and she buried her face against his chest, clinging to him as the sobs racked her body.

'Oh, lord, I didn't mean to upset you,' Cal groaned, holding her tightly against him. 'Helen, I'm sorry, so sorry.'

She wasn't, not really, Ben just something else that had stood between them. She had loved her brother dearly, had been more like the mother to him that he had never known, and she had found it impossible over the years to talk about him with anyone, even her father. *Especially* her father—both of them were too close to Ben. But she had known how much her father needed to talk of the baby they had lost, had regretted not being able to share that with him, even in words, knew that he had recognised an affinity in Cal that made it possible for him to talk to the younger man.

Helen now knew that same affinity.

She regained some control, shaking her head. 'It was so long ago.'

'That doesn't lessen the pain,' Cal said understandingly.

'It should have dulled it,' she returned firmly.

'You had a double tragedy of the magnitude most people couldn't even begin to imagine,' he soothed gruffly.

And he understood all too well what she had been through. In a way she had always known that he would, had feared even that closeness between them, could feel the tendrils of that known affinity wrapping themselves around her heart. She knew, and in a way, accepted, her physical attraction towards this man, but she didn't want to care for him any more deeply than that, was afraid to care for anyone in that way. And yet she knew that with this man she was dangerously close to doing just that.

She pulled out of his arms, making an obvious move away from him. 'It was all a long time ago,' she repeated firmly. 'So Daddy has offered to have Sam here while you're away?' she added briskly, the distance she had deliberately put between them not just one of proximity.

Cal looked as if he would have liked to have said more on the subject of Ben and her mother, but he could obviously tell by her expression that she wouldn't welcome any further intrusion upon her battered emotions.

'Yes,' he confirmed heavily. 'But if it's going to upset you . . . ?'

'Of course not,' she denied offhandedly, having no real idea just how Sam being in the house would affect her. 'I'm sure we'll cope very well. I can take him down on the beach during the day, I'm sure he would like that.'

'Yes,' Cal agreed distractedly. 'I'm going to sort out things with Enid and Henry once and for all, legally, if possible.'

After the other day Helen had a feeling that might be the only way he could stop the arguments! 'Poor Sam,' she sighed.

'I don't know what else to do to put a stop to all this,' Cal confided sadly. 'I do have an alternative, but—— Well, it isn't one I could ever use,' he dismissed hardly. 'Susan wouldn't have wanted me to do that. They left me a letter, you see,' he agitatedly paced the room. 'Explaining why it had to be me who had Sam.'

Helen had sensed there was something he was keeping to himself, felt uncomfortable at having him confide in her in this way, felt those tendrils about her emotions drawing in tighter.

'Susan loved her parents,' Cal continued heavily. 'But she knew they were the last people to bring up Sam. Susan was born to them late in life, was almost suffocated by them during her childhood; she couldn't bear the thought, much as she loved them, of their putting those same restrictions on Sam's life.'

So this was that other 'act of defiance' that Susan had committed, not openly as her marriage to Graham had needed to be, but quietly, privately, with the man they had entrusted their son's life to. It just made Helen feel all the worse for all the awful thoughts she had had of Cal since before she even arrived here a couple of weeks ago.

Was it really only two and a half weeks since she had first met this man? She was beginning to feel as if she had known him a lifetime!

And what she had just learnt of the trust that had been placed in Cal made a nonsense of all the bad things she had been imagining of him. And she could only admire him more for the restraint he was exercising concerning Enid Carter; it must be so tempting for him to just show the other woman the letter and stop her insults once and for all, and yet she knew Cal would never do that, that he would try to maintain the love the Carters had for their daughter no matter what the cost might be to himself. Although Helen was equally convinced that he wouldn't exercise that same constraint if Sam's welfare was to become really threatened.

It was a terrible, if necessary, burden that had been placed on him. And he had chosen to share that burden with her...

'I'd better go,' Cal decided suddenly, as if he too was slightly taken aback at having confided in her the way that he had. 'I'll be over early tomorrow with Sam. Is that going to be all right with you?' He looked at her anxiously.

She shrugged with much more nonchalance than she actually felt. 'It really isn't my decision; as my father is fond of pointing out, this is his house, not mine,' she said ruefully.

'Helen——'

'Cal, it will be all right,' she cut in tautly, her cheeks colouring slightly as she realised she had used that shortened version of his name for the first time. But then, their relationship had changed so drastically in the course of just one short evening that it wasn't surprising she was slightly off balance! 'It *will* be all right,' she repeated firmly.

He looked as if he would have liked to say more but restrained himself with effort. 'I'll see you in the morning, then,' he told her gruffly.

'Yes,' she acknowledged abruptly, walking out to the door, looking at him expectantly as he seemed reluctant to leave. 'I had better get some rest too if I'm to chase after Sam the next few days,' she said lightly. 'I'm sure that's what Daddy really had in mind when he made the offer!'

Cal seemed relieved that the tension had been lifted, smiling down at her. 'I wouldn't be at all surprised, although the two of them do get on well together.'

She sobered a little, knowing how much her father had regretted the fact that Ben had rarely been well enough to play with, let alone get into mischief the way Sam did. 'I'm sure.' She nodded curtly.

'Helen?'

She looked up at Cal warily. Her emotions were too ragged already; she couldn't stand much more tonight!

'Goodnight.' His lips lightly brushed her own before he left, seeming to sense her vulnerability and not want to take advantage of it.

Helen stayed in the lounge a long time after he had gone, tired and yet not sleepy, knowing that the next few days were going to be a severe strain on her emotions.

'Asleep?' her father asked indulgently as she came down the stairs.

She had just fed Sam his tea, bathed him, put him to bed, and read him a story, which he had fallen asleep halfway through. So much for that story of Rapunzel that Cal had said he liked; she had a feeling Cal enjoyed that story more than the baby did!

As she had thought would happen, she had looked after Sam more than her father had, her father seeming to think he only had to play with the little boy a couple of times a day and that he would amuse and look after himself the rest of the time. Admittedly it was a long time since her father had had a young child in the house, but he seemed to have forgotten all the other things there were to taking care of one! If he had ever known. Helen seemed to recall that her mother had done most of the looking after when she was young; before his early retirement last year her father had been kept busy with the clothing store he had owned and run in the nearby town.

After only three days of running about after Sam Helen was exhausted, dropping down tiredly into one of the armchairs.

'Yes, he is, thank good——' She broke off as the telephone rang, groaning at the thought of getting up to answer it. 'Would you?' she asked her father wearily.

He glanced at his wristwatch. 'It will only be for you,' he said derisively.

If one of them didn't answer it soon then neither of them would need to!

'It's eight o'clock,' her father added pointedly, teasing humour in his eyes.

She stood up with an impatient frown in her father's direction.

'Cal doesn't telephone at eight o'clock every night to talk to me,' her father taunted as she went out into the hallway to answer the still ringing telephone.

'He's checking on Sam,' she turned briefly to snap irritably.

'Of course he is,' came her father's taunting reply as Helen picked up the receiver.

'Everything all right?' came Cal's anxious voice down the line.

Her father was right about these calls; they had come regularly at this time for the previous two evenings too. He was also right that Cal didn't call to talk to him; he always enquired after Sam in great detail, but he also made it obvious that he wanted to hear her voice too.

'Fine,' she answered lightly, going on in some detail about the events of Sam's day. 'He wants to know when you're coming home.' Those deep blue eyes had filled up with tears today when Sam had asked where his uncle was. And she had to admit, though not because she was tired of looking after Sam, that she would be interested in knowing herself when Cal intended coming back. Much as she hated to admit it, she had missed him.

'Tomorrow,' Cal answered with some relief. 'I'm not absolutely sure what time. But everything is sorted out with Enid and Henry at last.'

'Without——'

'Yes, without that,' Cal confirmed dismissively. 'Enid has been suffering with her nerves for some time, and I finally managed to persuade Henry to get her doctor to advise her that rest and no pressure are what she needs now. Henry has never wanted to interfere in Sam's custody anyway, so he was only too pleased to try and calm the situation down; it was just a question of seeing him on my own for a time and sorting out a plan of action. I'm not saying Enid won't still be a pain, but I think she's finally been convinced that she isn't strong enough to take care of a very young child.'

It also meant that Enid Carter had a very valid excuse, for herself as much as anyone else, for not pressing to have Sam with her. None of that really mattered as long as Sam could now be left in peace to settle down to life with the uncle he obviously adored.

'I'm glad.' And they both knew she didn't just mean the custody of Sam, that she was also relieved that it hadn't been necessary to use Susan's letter to achieve the armed truce that now existed between Cal and Sam's grandparents.

'Can you take Sam back to the house tomorrow?' Cal's voice was husky, knowing exactly what she had meant by her statement.

Daniel was at the house. She had seen him about the estate several times when she'd taken Sam down to the beach, had studiously avoided actually being close enough to have to acknowledge him.

'Couldn't you pick him up from here?' she suggested tautly.

'I'm really not sure how early or late I'll be,' Cal answered in a preoccupied voice. 'But if there's a problem with your going to the house——'

BIG SUMMER READ

Summer Reading At Its Best

In July, Harlequin and Silhouette bring readers the Big Summer Read Program. Heat up your summer with these four exciting new novels by top Harlequin and Silhouette authors.

SOMEWHERE IN TIME by Barbara Bretton
YESTERDAY COMES TOMORROW by Rebecca Flanders
A DAY IN APRIL by Mary Lynn Baxter
LOVE CHILD by Patricia Coughlin

From time travel to fame and fortune, this program offers something for everyone.

Available at your favorite retail outlet.

FREE GIFT OFFER

With Free Gift Promotion proofs-of-purchase from Harlequin or Silhouette, you can receive this beautiful jewelry collection. Each item is perfect by itself, or collect all three for a complete jewelry ensemble.

For a classic look that is always in style, this beautiful gold tone jewelry will complement any outfit. Items include:

Gold tone clip earrings (approx. retail value $9.95), a 7½" gold tone bracelet (approx. retail value $15.95) and a 18" gold tone necklace (approx. retail value $29.95).

FREE GIFT OFFER TERMS

To receive your free gift, complete the certificate according to directions. Be certain to enclose the required number of Free Gift proofs-of-purchase, which are found on the last page of every specially marked Free Gift Harlequin or Silhouette romance novel. Requests must be received no later than July 31, 1992. Items depicted are for illustrative purposes only and may not be exactly as shown. Please allow 6 to 8 weeks for receipt of order. Offer good while quantities of gifts last. In the event an ordered gift is no longer available, you will receive a free, previously unpublished Harlequin or Silhouette book for every proof-of-purchase you have submitted with your request, plus a refund of the postage-and-handling charge you have included. Offer good in the U.S. and Canada only.

'There's no problem,' she cut in sharply. 'As long as you make sure we're expected.' The last thing she wanted was to run into Daniel unexpectedly; there was no telling what his reaction to seeing her again might be, and it might be done in front of witnesses!

'I'll ring the housekeeper and confirm that with her,' Cal instantly assured her. 'How are you?' His voice was husky now.

Her cheeks felt hot. 'Very well.' Better than she had expected, actually; Sam was a joy to have around rather than a constant reminder of Ben, as she had thought he might be. Sam brought with him only joy and laughter, whereas any joy and laughter she had known with Ben had been tinged with the knowledge that he would be with them for only a short time; Sam was bright sunshine, whereas Ben had been like a bright star in the sky. There *was* no comparison.

'I'm glad,' Cal said softly. 'Will you have dinner at the house with me tomorrow night?'

Daniel was there, she reminded herself once again, although the hunger to be with Cal again warred with that knowledge.

'There won't be anyone there but the two of us.' Cal seemed to guess—if not necessarily for the right reason!—her reluctance to see Daniel at the house again. 'Daniel isn't returning from town until Monday morning.'

Daniel hadn't gone to London with Cal, but he must have returned there for his weekend off. His absence took away any last lingering doubt she might have had about having dinner with Cal.

'I'd like that,' she accepted softly.

'I've missed you, Helen,' he told her huskily.

She had missed him too, although there was no way she was going to admit as much, even if he couldn't actually see the blush to her cheeks. 'I'll see you tomorrow some time,' she answered briskly.

Cal gave a husky laugh, seeming to guess how she felt without her actually having to speak a word. 'Give Sam a kiss for me,' he said lightly. 'And take one for yourself too,' he added softly before ringing off.

'Cal OK?' her father looked up from the newspaper to enquire.

'Did I say the call was from him?' She hadn't forgiven him for his earlier teasing yet!

'Only one person I know can bring that flush to your cheeks,' he mocked with affection.

Helen gave an impatient sigh. 'You'll be pleased to know that Cal is coming home tomorrow.'

'And are you pleased?'

'Daddy——'

'Strike that question.' He put the newspaper down to hold up his hands defensively. 'I can tell by your face that you're pleased,' he added teasingly, giving her a cheeky grin as she threw a cushion at him, catching it neatly in his hands. 'I'm pleased the two of you are getting on so much better.' He sobered, putting the cushion down. 'It was what I had hoped for.'

Helen gave him a considering look. 'What do you mean, it was what you had hoped for?' she questioned slowly.

He shrugged. 'I thought the two of you would get on together.'

'Yes?' She was very still now.

'There's nothing wrong with that,' he said defensively at her accusing look. 'You're my only daughter, and I happen to like Cal very much.'

'Yes?' she prompted again, more than a little wary now.

'Nothing else.' He stood up agitatedly. 'I just wanted the two of you to like each other.'

'We like each other,' she admitted slowly, a suspicion suddenly hitting her. 'Daddy——'

'That's good then, isn't it?' he dismissed lightly.

'That depends,' Helen said consideringly.

Her father was starting to look uncomfortable. 'I don't know——'

'Just how far were you prepared to go in order for Cal and I to "get on"?' she cut in in a hard voice.

'Helen——'

'How far, Daddy?' she repeated with firm determination.

He stood up agitatedly, pacing the room, not at all happy with the turn the conversation had taken.

'Daddy——'

'Oh, all right,' he snapped impatiently. 'So I exaggerated a little about wanting to sell Cherry Trees to Cal, but it turned out all right in the end, didn't it?' He faced her defiantly.

She couldn't believe he had done this to her, didn't want to believe he was capable of such a thing, and yet she knew that he was.

No wonder Cal was so stunned by her attacks on him for wanting to buy this house; the sale hadn't been his idea at all, he hadn't really been interested in buying it!

She could see it all now, knew exactly what her father had done, realised that he had brought her down here in the first place under false pretences, in anger if that was the only way to achieve his objective; he had wanted her and Cal to 'get on'. But for what purpose?

'Did it?' she rasped hardly.

'Now look, Helen——'

'I'm trying to, Daddy.' She nodded slowly.

'Cal's a good man,' he defended stubbornly.

She had come round to that idea herself, even more so since she had realised the lengths he was prepared to go to, the insults he had been willing to put up with, in order to avoid hurting Enid Carter. The man she had first thought Cal to be wouldn't have cared whom he hurt as long as he achieved his objective.

Cal hadn't said a word either to disabuse her of her belief that he was after Cherry Trees in an underhand way, by using his friendship with her father. Now it turned out that her *father* had been using the friendship to try and matchmake between the two of them.

Had Cal realised that?

If he had, why hadn't he put her firmly in her place when she had begun to insult him?

She remembered the things he had said to her earlier, the times she had been in his arms. What did it all mean?

She was afraid to hope.

'I'm just beginning to realise how good,' she reproved her father. 'He must have realised long ago what you were up to.' She shook her head disgustedly.

'It didn't put him off, did it?' he said with satisfaction. 'On the contrary,' he added pointedly.

'Well, now that we *both* know what you've been up to you can just stop it,' she snapped in her agitation. 'Forget about selling Cherry Trees and just stop your interfering,' she said warningly.

'I was only thinking of you, Helen——'

'Were you?' she cut in derisively.

He had the grace to look slightly uncomfortable. 'Maybe not completely,' he admitted ruefully. 'Maybe I am being selfish in wanting you to be happy, with a family of your own. But I wanted it for you as much as for me.'

'You're assuming rather a lot.' Her cheeks were hot with embarrassment.

'You can't blame me for trying,' he reasoned imploringly.

No, maybe she couldn't blame him for that. She just wished she had been more aware of what he had been up to from the first, then she possibly wouldn't have made such a fool of herself over Cherry Trees. Cal must think she was a shrew.

But that *hadn't* stopped him wanting to be with her, taking her in his arms, that little voice in her brain kept persisting.

'Couldn't you have just introduced the two of us and left the rest to chance?' she sighed.

'You're always so defensive with men, keep them at such a distance, that Cal would probably never have got past that wall you put up around yourself,' her father explained. 'This way, you were both thrown slightly off guard.'

He was right; she knew he was right. But even so...

'Just don't ever do anything like this again,' she cautioned.

He eyed her speculatively. 'Will I need to?'

Helen didn't even bother to answer him, starting to collect up Sam's toys ready to take him home tomorrow.

Would he need to?

'Well, well, well,' drawled a mocking voice. 'So you've brought the little cherub back, have you?'

Helen spun round from unpacking Sam's toys in the nursery—the baby was asleep in the adjoining bedroom—getting up to gently close the door between the two rooms before answering Daniel's taunting remark.

She had returned to the house mid-morning, having lunch with Sam downstairs before putting him down for his afternoon nap. Daniel had obviously returned from London earlier than Cal had expected!

He seemed to be working, dressed in a suit and pristine white shirt, his golden hair meticulous. He left Helen cold.

'Sam is back home, yes,' she replied in a controlled voice.

Daniel strolled further into the room, his gaze flickering over her insolently, the pale yellow sun-dress she wore and her loosened hair obviously finding approval as his gaze warmed speculatively.

'I must say you're a dark horse, Helen,' he taunted. 'No wonder I didn't get very far with you—you were saving yourself for a much bigger fish!'

Two spots of angry colour darkened her cheeks. 'Don't judge everyone by your own standards! It's almost six years since I knew you; if I were as mercenary as you're implying I would have found someone rich by now!'

Daniel shrugged, strolling carelessly round the room. 'Maybe you weren't in a hurry.'

'And maybe I wasn't looking for anyone rich at all!' she snapped contemptuously.

'But you seem to have found him,' Daniel drawled pointedly.

'Cal is a friend of my father's——'

'Oh, come on, Helen,' Daniel scoffed. 'I saw the two of you together the other evening.'

'You didn't see anything,' she dismissed hardly.

He shrugged. 'Maybe if I had delayed my entrance a little longer I might have done!'

'That's disgusting!' she gasped with distaste for the unpleasantness of this man's mind. Had she really once found him attractive? She found that impossible to believe now, although she hadn't really seen this side of him until she had thwarted his intentions towards her almost six years ago—up until that moment he had been nothing but charm and warmth.

'Oh, don't be such a prude, Helen,' he derided impatiently. 'We don't have to play games any more; you're out for what you can get out of life and so am I.' He shrugged. 'I have a healthy respect for anyone who doesn't mind admitting that.'

Helen eyed him with dislike. 'There's nothing healthy about having that attitude towards people,' she scorned.

'I told you, you don't have to play games any more,' he chided softly. 'And who knows, maybe we can have a little fun together as well?'

She stiffened. 'What do you mean?'

'You can't be that näive,' he mocked, moving towards her, taking her into his arms. 'I always wanted you, Helen.' His arms tightened as she struggled against him. 'I think it's all this cool "don't touch me!" beauty that does it,' he added appreciatively.

'Let go of me!' She pushed against his chest. How dared he touch her in this way?

'I told you,' he murmured softly. 'You don't have to pretend any more.'

'I'm not *pretending* the disgust I feel for you!' She still pushed against his chest, although couldn't manage to free herself completely.

His face hardened. 'Let's put it another way, Helen,' he said with soft menace. 'Neither of us wants Cal to realise we knew each other six years ago, but *I* only have a job to lose . . .'

Helen became very still, looking up at him disbelievingly. 'Are you trying to blackmail me into going to bed with you?' She was incredulous at the idea of it.

'Blackmail is a little too strong a word,' he dismissed lightly. 'I——'

'I don't think it's too strong at all,' rasped a familiar voice from the open doorway into the hallway.

Helen turned to look at Cal with open horror, not having been aware of his presence in the house because of her argument with Daniel.

CHAPTER TEN

BY THE time Cal had come further into the room, his eyes a cold metallic blue in his anger, Helen had released herself and moved as far away from Daniel as she could possibly get, her legs trembling, her hands shaking.

She couldn't believe this was happening. *Could* it really be?

Cal glared at the other man with cold fury. 'I want your things packed and you out of my house in half an hour.'

'Half an hour?' Daniel gasped indignantly. 'But——'

'Think yourself lucky I'm giving you that long,' Cal bit out tautly, obviously controlling himself with effort. 'If it weren't for the fact that I don't want any reminder of you left in the house I'd make you go right now and send your things on to you.'

'Look, Cal——'

'Will you just go?' he rasped. 'Before I do something you'll regret.' The physical threat was obvious. Cal looked at the other man with open contempt. '*I* certainly wouldn't regret it.'

'Helen and I are old friends,' Daniel persisted cajolingly, ignoring her outraged gasp as he looked at the other man for understanding, finding only a cold stare in return. 'I realise it must have sounded bad to you when you arrived, but——'

'It didn't sound bad, Scott,' Cal bit out between clenched teeth. 'It sounded exactly what it was, and I don't even begin to deal with blackmailers. Now get out.'

Daniel looked at the other man for several seconds, finally realising that he wasn't going to get anywhere with him, throwing Helen a vindictive look before turning back to Cal. 'Helen and I were lovers long ago——'

'That isn't true!' she cried out desperately, looking to Cal to believe her. He still looked at Daniel, his expression enigmatic. 'It isn't true,' she repeated lamely. 'We did know each other, but——'

'Would you leave, Helen?' Cal instructed in an even voice, still not looking at her.

He didn't believe her. Oh, lord, this couldn't be happening!

'Cal, please,' she choked, looking at him imploringly.

'Helen, leave,' he told her through gritted teeth.

She felt sick, running from the room with a choked cry.

She had known, the moment she first saw him in the nursery doorway, that she had fallen irrevocably in love with Caleb Jones!

'Love, wouldn't it help to talk about it?' her father prompted gently.

She had stopped crying now, just felt completely numb, sitting on the edge of her bed, her face as white as the sheets she sat on.

She was too numbed to talk, her emotions a vacuum.

'Helen?' he prompted again, his arms about her shoulders, looking at her with worried concern.

She shook her head. 'It's—it's too awful.' She swallowed hard, the nausea having got worse, not better.

'Tell me.'

She still couldn't talk about that awful scene at Cal's house, didn't even know how she had got home or up to her bedroom. She had just wanted to be alone with her pain.

Her father had followed her up the stairs, had sat beside her with worried concern while she cried as if she would never stop. But she had to stop eventually and when she did her father was still there, waiting to be of what comfort to her that he could.

She loved Cal.

It was fact, indisputable; she had known it the moment she'd realised he was standing in the doorway looking at her in Daniel's arms.

And he didn't even want her in the same house as him, had just wanted her away from him as quickly as possible.

She couldn't tell her father about that, couldn't bear him to know of Cal's disgust with her.

'It might help to talk about it,' her father encouraged.

The old, well-worn platitude. As if it ever really did help in a situation like this. It couldn't make Cal's disgust with her go away.

'No,' she said flatly.

'Helen——' He broke off as the doorbell rang. 'Damn,' he muttered as he stood up. 'I'll be back as soon as I can,' he promised concernedly.

If that was Daniel come to gloat because he had managed to ruin her life once again she didn't think she would be answerable for the consequences!

She could hear the door being opened, the murmur of voices, the door closing again, then silence.

At least it wasn't Daniel—it couldn't have been or her father would have been more heated than he had been.

She turned back into her bedroom, her movements heavy with despair.

'Helen.'

She turned sharply at the sound of Cal's voice. What did he want? Had he come here to tell her exactly what he thought of her and her past association with Daniel? But it hadn't been what he thought it was! Not that that would make much difference, she had still deceived him about not knowing Daniel at all.

He looked at her closely. 'Your father said you're upset.'

'I——' She swallowed hard. 'I'm all right now,' she lied; she didn't think she would ever be all right again.

'I'm sorry all that, at the house, had to happen,' Cal sighed.

'So am I.' She nodded.

How could she have ever thought she disliked this man? How could she ever have mistrusted him? He was now more dear to her, more important than anything else in her life had ever been. And it was too late. Just too damned late.

'Scott is a very unpleasant man,' Cal said with distaste. 'I don't know how I could ever have been fooled by him for a moment.' He shook his head with self-disgust.

'Nor I,' Helen said heavily.

'I doubt either of us will ever see him again,' Cal told her with satisfaction, his expression grim. 'I made my opinion of him pretty clear after you had gone.'

She moistened dry lips, nodding. 'I see.'

Had he come here to do the same to her? She didn't think she could bear it, even if the attack was perfectly justifiable, if he was to tell her exactly what he thought of her too!

'Helen, I know all that was—unpleasant, for you, but it's over now. There's no use upsetting yourself about it any more,' he calmed gently.

She swallowed hard. 'I couldn't believe it when I discovered he was the man you had taken on.'

'No,' Cal grimaced. 'It must have been a shock for you.'

Helen looked at him with pained green eyes. 'I don't know what he told you about our relationship in the past but I can assure you I wanted nothing more to do with him once I realised how underhand his dealings were.' She had to at least disabuse him of that point.

'He tried to tell a different tale.' Cal nodded. 'But I wasn't going to fall for that.'

'You weren't?' She looked at him in sudden hope.

'Of course not,' he denied contemptuously. 'I know you, Helen, you aren't that sort of person at all. Lord, woman,' a sudden thought seemed to have occurred to him, 'you didn't think I actually believed the man, did you?'

'You seemed—um—you didn't want me near you,' she reminded shakily, remembering the pain of that moment.

'I wanted you away from there before I began to pull Scott apart limb from limb!' he corrected incredulously. 'You didn't really believe I asked you to leave because I couldn't bear you near me?' he gasped disbelievingly. 'Oh, Helen, I've never wanted to hold you more, to be with you more; I missed you like hell while I was away. But I had to deal with Scott, and if he had said much more about you while you had to stand there listening to the lies I would have hit him then and there!'

'You would?' she gasped.

'I would,' he confirmed teasingly, crossing the room to her side.

Helen looked up at him with wide eyes. 'How do you know they were lies?'

Cal gave her a reproving look. 'I'm not even going to acknowledge the stupidity of that question by answering it,' he dismissed firmly.

'But——'

'Helen, all the way back from London today I was thinking about kissing you.' His gaze on her lips was almost like a caress. 'Nothing else, just kissing you.'

Her breath seemed caught in her throat. 'Cal——'

'Nothing else, Helen,' he repeated, his arms closing firmly about her. 'Not Sam. Not the estate. Not work. Just kissing you.'

She didn't want to argue with that, just wanted to be in his arms, returning that kiss he seemed to want so badly. It didn't seem possible, after what she had believed earlier, but if Cal said it was so then it was.

'Please—kiss me,' she groaned her own need, her body curved into his.

They were both desperate for the contact, their days apart, plus that awful scene earlier, having heightened their need of each other. The kiss went on and on, neither wanting it to end.

Cal finally pulled back with a husky laugh. 'This had better stop, or we'll have David coming upstairs to break us apart.'

Helen shakily returned his smile, knowing that if he hadn't stopped then she wouldn't have cared whether her father had interrupted them or not. Although he was probably consumed with curiosity as he waited downstairs!

'I love you, Helen,' Cal told her gruffly.

She swallowed hard. 'But—you hardly know me,' she said breathlessly, hardly able to believe this was happening to her.

'All the details can wait,' he dismissed indulgently. 'I love *you*, the person I know you to be, the woman who allowed Sam into her life despite the pain it caused you.' They sat down on the bed, Cal's arm about her shoulder. 'I knew from the very first moment I realised you were David's daughter how deeply being with Sam affected you. Just as I knew I wanted you in my life,' he added softly.

'I was rude and arrogant at our first meeting,' she said disbelievingly.

'With good reason,' he defended. 'I still get the shakes when I think of what might have happened. And I know that it was just as traumatic for you.'

Oh, it had been. The whole incident could have had tragic consequences.

'I do love you, Helen,' Cal turned to her intensely, instantly banishing the memory of that near disaster when they had first met. 'I love you and I want to marry you. If you'll have me.'

'What?' she gasped.

'I want you as my wife, Helen,' he told her deeply. 'If you could learn to love me. Hell, even if you can't love me,' he added desperately. 'We could have a good life together, Helen. And you do respond to me, that's enough to be going on with.'

She drew in a steadying breath. 'If this is for Sam's sake——'

'It's for *my* sake,' he cut in with impatient anger. 'Haven't you listened to a word I've been saying? I love you; I want to marry you. I've lived thirty-nine years without feeling the emotion; give me the credit of being able to recognise it when it at last comes into my life! And yes, it would be nice for Sam to have a mother figure in his life, but it isn't going to be the end of the world if he doesn't. I don't want to marry you for Sam, I want to marry you because, quite honestly, the thought of having to live without you now is a desperate one!'

She had to believe him, could see the naked pain in those dark blue eyes. 'I love you too,' she choked. 'I didn't want to——'

'I would never have guessed that!' Cal murmured affectionately.

'It hurts too much to love, Cal.' She swallowed hard.

'But it gives much more than it takes away,' he encouraged eagerly. 'Yes, we'll argue. Yes, we'll probably hurt each other. But at the end of all that we'll still have each other and the love we feel for each other. I still can't believe you feel the same way I do!' He shook his head dazedly.

How could she not have loved this man? She had been sure to lose this battle from the first, and should have realised that. But if she had she would never have gone near him, and the thought now of living without this burning excitement of loving him and being loved in return was a devastating one.

'Daddy planned for this to happen, you know,' she felt bound to say.

'I knew that,' Cal nodded ruefully. 'And at first his matchmaking amused me. I had no intention of buying Cherry Trees from him until he brought the subject up——'

'Oh, I realise that.' She sighed at her father's duplicity.

'But I only had to meet you the once to decide his matchmaking was a good idea.' He grinned. 'There's nothing like having a father's approval before you've even met the lady concerned!'

'He's incorrigible!' Her cheeks were flushed with embarrassment. 'If I had known what he was up to in the beginning I never would have come down here.'

'And that would have been a tragedy,' Cal said heavily.

Yes, it would. But even so... 'You do realise that he'll be interfering like this for the rest of our lives,' she cautioned.

'"Rest of our lives"?' Cal looked at her with a burning hunger in his eyes.

Her heart beat a wild tattoo in her chest, her pulse racing. 'I never thought I would say this to anyone,' she could barely speak now for nerves, 'but I would love to marry you.'

'I have a ready-made family,' he pointed out reluctantly. 'Not many women would want to take that on.' He looked at her anxiously.

Helen gave a choked laugh. 'I would want to marry you if you had half a dozen children already—as long as they were all as adorable as Sam!'

His arms tightened about her, his face buried in her hair. '*Our* children will be as adorable as Sam. More so probably, with the beautiful mother they are going to have.'

Their children.

Even in her wildest imaginings that was something she had never dreamt of.

'Shh, you have to be very quiet.' She could hear Cal whispering to Sam, smiling dreamily to herself as she pictured them creeping into the room so that they shouldn't disturb her.

She opened one eye in the semi-darkness, watching them as they crossed the room to her bedside, the tall strong man and the sturdy three-year-old at his side.

Sam had grown a lot the last two years, looking even more like Cal as he matured, taking on a lot of his uncle's characteristics too as he copied the man he adored.

He peered now over the side of the crib that stood at Helen's bedside, frowning deeply. 'She's very small, Uncle Cal.'

Cal gave a throaty laugh, ruffling the little boy's hair. 'You were that small once, Sam.'

Sam gave him a scoffing look that clearly doubted that, before turning back to the crib. 'I can't see her properly; is she pretty?'

'Not as pretty as her mother——'

'Flattery will get you everywhere, Cal Jones.' Helen laughed softly as she sat up in the bed and switched on the bedside lamp, blushing at the unashamed adoration in Cal's eyes as he looked down at her.

In the early hours of that morning they had shared the experience of seeing their daughter come into the world, her thick blonde hair the same colour as her mother's, the eyes looking as if they would stay the deep blue of her father's. No couple could share a more beautiful moment than seeing their child born.

'We didn't wake you?' Cal leant down to brush his lips against her, his gaze full of tenderness.

She shook her head. 'I was only dozing. So what do you think of her, Sam?' she prompted teasingly.

He gave the baby a considering look as she lay so peacefully asleep, long dark lashes fanned out across her peachy cream cheeks;

after all the warnings she had had of babies looking all red and wrinkled, little Elizabeth was the most beautiful baby Helen could ever have imagined.

'I thought I'd be able to play with her,' he voiced his main disappointment.

'You will, when she's older.' Helen gave Cal a conspiratorial smile before turning her attention back on the little boy. 'I did try to explain that to you, Sam, before she was born.'

'Yes.' But he sounded as if he had hoped she might be mistaken about it, and now that he had seen the baby his worst fears had been confirmed.

Cal laughed softly, swinging Sam up into his arms, looking nothing at all like a man who had spent most of the night holding Helen's hand through the labour of birth, euphoria making him look years younger. 'She'll get bigger, Sam,' he consoled the little boy.

Sam didn't look very convinced about that, but now that he had seen how boring the baby was going to be he decided he would explore Helen's hospital room, asking to be put down before wandering off.

Cal sat on the side of the bed. 'How are you feeling?' Concern for her darkened his eyes.

'Wonderful!' she assured him warmly, clasping his hand in hers.

'David can hardly wait to see her,' Cal told her ruefully. 'He should be along later.'

She smiled indulgently, knowing how pleased her father would be that they had named the baby after her mother.

The last two years had been the happiest Helen had ever known, happiness beyond her imagining. As Cal had predicted, they did have their arguments, but the making up had always been worth it!

And now they had a daughter to complete their happiness; Sam was already like a son to them both, so Elizabeth had been like a completion of their family unit.

Helen sat up with a smile as the baby began to stir, wondering what Sam was going to make of her feeding the baby herself.

Cal bent down to pick the baby up, the hard planes of his face softened with tenderness for his little daughter. 'I'm not going to stand a chance with two of you in the house,' he said ruefully, placing the baby in her waiting arms. 'Sam and I will have to try very hard to resist the pair of you!'

Helen touched the tiny hand that lay so trustingly against her breast, her eyes full of unshed tears as she looked at Cal. 'I love you very much, my darling. Thank you so much for loving me.'

'Thank *you*,' he said gruffly, as moved by the moment as she was.

Sam climbed up on the bed with them, watching the baby with more interest now.

As she looked at her family all around her Helen knew she had never known a moment of such sheer happiness before. She didn't doubt for a single second that the happiness would continue . . .

HARLEQUIN
Romance®

announces

THE BRIDAL COLLECTION

one special Romance
every month,
featuring
a Bride, a Groom and a Wedding!

Beginning in May 1992
with
The Man You'll Marry
by Debbie Macomber

WED-1

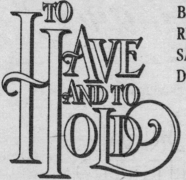

FREE GIFT OFFER

To receive your free gift, send us the specified number of proofs-of-purchase from any specially marked Free Gift Offer Harlequin or Silhouette book with the Free Gift Certificate properly completed, plus a check or money order (do not send cash) to cover postage and handling payable to Harlequin/Silhouette Free Gift Promotion Offer. We will send you the specified gift.

FREE GIFT CERTIFICATE

ITEM	A. GOLD TONE EARRINGS	B. GOLD TONE BRACELET	C. GOLD TONE NECKLACE
# of proofs-of-purchase required	3	6	9
Postage and Handling	$2.25	$2.75	$3.25
Check one	☐	☐	☐

Name: _____

Address: _____

City: _____ Province: _____ Postal Code: _____

Mail this certificate, specified number of proofs-of-purchase and a check or money order for postage and handling to: HARLEQUIN/SILHOUETTE FREE GIFT OFFER 1992, P.O. Box 622, Fort Erie, Ontario L2A 5X3. Requests must be received by July 31, 1992.

PLUS—Every time you submit a completed certificate with the correct number of proofs-of-purchase, you are automatically entered in our MILLION DOLLAR SWEEPSTAKES! No purchase or obligation necessary to enter. See below for alternate means of entry and how to obtain complete sweepstakes rules.

MILLION DOLLAR SWEEPSTAKES
NO PURCHASE OR OBLIGATION NECESSARY TO ENTER

To enter, hand-print (mechanical reproductions are not acceptable) your name and address on a 3″×5″ card and mail to Million Dollar Sweepstakes 6097, c/o either P.O. Box 9056, Buffalo, NY 14269-9056 or P.O. Box 621, Fort Erie, Ontario L2A 5X3. Limit: one entry per envelope. Entries must be sent via 1st-class mail. For eligibility, entries must be received no later than March 31, 1994. No liability is assumed for printing errors, lost, late or misdirected entries.

Sweepstakes is open to persons 18 years of age or older. All applicable laws and regulations apply. Sweepstakes offer void wherever prohibited by law. Prizewinners will be determined no later than May 1994. Chances of winning are determined by the number of entries distributed and received. For a copy of the Official Rules governing this sweepstakes offer, send a self-addressed, stamped envelope (WA residents need not affix return postage) to: Million Dollar Sweepstakes Rules, P.O. Box 4733, Blair, NE 68009.

✂ HP1C

ONE PROOF-OF-PURCHASE

To collect your fabulous FREE GIFT you must include the necessary FREE GIFT proofs-of-purchase with a properly completed offer certificate.

(See center insert for details)

® Harlequin ®

JANELLE TAYLOR

Valley of Fire

HARLEQUIN IS PROUD TO PRESENT *VALLEY OF FIRE* BY JANELLE TAYLOR—AUTHOR OF TWENTY-TWO BOOKS, INCLUDING SIX *NEW YORK TIMES* BESTSELLERS

VALLEY OF FIRE—the warm and passionate story of Kathy Alexander, a famous romance author, and Steven Winngate, entrepreneur and owner of the magazine that intended to expose the real Kathy "Brandy" Alexander to her fans.

Don't miss VALLEY OF FIRE, available in May.

Take 4 bestselling love stories FREE

Plus get a FREE surprise gift!

HARLEQUIN Temptation

Rebels & Rogues

Quinn: He was a real-life hero to everyone except himself.

THE MIGHTY QUINN
by Candace Schuler
Temptation #397, June 1992

All men are not created equal. Some are rough around the edges. Tough-minded but tenderhearted. Incredibly sexy. The tempting fulfillment of every woman's fantasy.

When it's time to fight for what they believe in, to win that special woman, our Rebels and Rogues are heroes at heart. Twelve Rebels and Rogues, one each month in 1992, only from Harlequin Temptation!